DARK SCIENCE FICTION
SHORT STORIES

DARK SCIENCE FICTION SHORT STORIES

LARRY BOTKINS

gatekeeper press
Where Authors are Family
Columbus, Ohio

This book is a work of fiction. The names, characters and events in this book are the products of the author's imagination or are used fictitiously. Any similarity to real persons living or dead is coincidental and not intended by the author.

Dark Science Fiction Short Stories

Published by Gatekeeper Press
2167 Stringtown Rd, Suite 109
Columbus, OH 43123-2989
www.GatekeeperPress.com

Copyright © 2019 by Larry Botkins
All rights reserved. Neither this book, nor any parts within it may be sold or reproduced in any form or by any electronic or mechanical means, including information storage and retrieval systems without permission in writing from the author. The only exception is by a reviewer, who may quote short excerpts in a review.

ISBN (paperback): 9781642374995
eISBN: 9781642375008

Printed in the United States of America

TABLE OF CONTENTS

The Reloader..7

The Confession 39

Eternal War 63

Planet of Idiots... 85

Rain of Death.. 145

The Protectors... 161

THE RELOADER

I've been reloading pistol and rifle ammunition for many years, and that hobby became the centerpiece in this story.

My equipment includes a Lee hand reloading press, which makes for a small, portable reloading kit. Normally, that kit travels no further than a comfortable chair, with some kind of mild entertainment nearby. Usually it's an old movie I've seen before which doesn't demand my full attention. After all, distractions could be unsafe while reloading ammunition!

I've sometimes wondered: could that portable kit be taken outside the house for some practical use elsewhere? Could something like that be used to reload ammunition for wartime use? It has happened before, as the story indicates. But what conditions would make such a thing necessary again, or even possible?

As always, history might provide an answer. It certainly wouldn't be a Stalingrad, where any room in any building could become a battlefield at any time. But what about a Leningrad? With shortages of everything, a shortage of ammunition could be conceivable. But even so, how would/could one possibly tell the story of reloading within a science fiction story?

Certainly Leningrad is an extreme example. But history is full of sieges and any one of them couldn't have been anything short of horrible. And with Orwell's works often in my thoughts lately, the possibilities for horror seem endless.

So if one endeavored to combine some of these monstrosities, what would it be like? What would it be like <u>here</u>?

DARK SCIENCE FICTION

WARNING:

Reloading data and procedures are present in this story only for the purpose of presenting a work of fiction. The data and procedures described herein are NOT to be used for reloading ammunition. Instead, reloading data and procedures should be taken only from the applicable equipment, component, or material manufacturer's publications; and from relevant documents or manuals published by established and competent organizations within the reloading, ammunition, and firearms industries. Otherwise, damage to property, severe injury, or even death may result.

I woke before the ration truck came, as I often had since the end of summer. Hunger made for light sleeping; cold made it brief. I remained on my mattress, within the warmth of my filthy sleeping bag. I rolled, with the bag, toward the street side of the building to better hear the ration truck's imminent approach. Almost reflexively, I gathered the looseness of the bag around me to hoard every bit of warmth.

Today was to be a very special day, with the alien coming. I had been told of that only at dinner call last night, when the Building Leader told me to prepare by cleaning my clothes and my apartment. But there wasn't much I could do. The clothes I was wearing were all I had and I'd never had running water in the apartment. Or gas, or electricity. Just off-white walls and beige carpet, all gradually growing more faded and dusty. All I could do was pick up some of the little bits of trash from the floor and arrange my reloading table.

As I had countless times, I longed again for the times before the aliens came, before the war against the aliens suddenly morphed into a civil war, and before the siege. And certainly before I was assigned this empty, always too-hot or too-cold apartment in Newport News, now an enclosed work-at-home compound. Life was so much better then, though I didn't appreciate it nearly enough. What fools we had been, fixated only on trivia.

Thoughts of food again. Pancakes in the morning, which I made from scratch, with either lots of cinnamon or ginger. My wife loved ginger pancakes with real maple syrup. Sometimes there was bacon and eggs, sometimes sausage and gravy, sometimes oatmeal and fruit. Always coffee. My wife always made the coffee, so strong and so hot. I missed her, and I missed coffee. She was declared "surplus" when we drove east to avoid the Red panic, and hadn't been picked up as a Worker. I became a Worker, it turned out, only because my box of portable reloading tools was found in the back of my Jeep, and I was quick to state that I knew how to use them. Some of those tools were there on the table. But as always, anything beyond the minimum required to support the war effort had been confiscated.

Finally, I heard the makeshift bell on the ration truck, ringing at the first two apartment buildings. The bell was a steel ring, apparently a truck wheel rim, hanging on a chain at the back of the ration truck. One of the ration crew beat the rim with his piece of steel pipe, which he also carried to guard the rations and the ration bearers. The bell was our signal to be up and ready.

My building and the one across the street were the second pair of buildings on the route. So I rolled out of my bag, off the mattress, and turned on my aching knees. I opened the bag fully and spread it across the mattress so the inside of the bag might dry during the day. The inside of it was getting smellier and stickier, which I hated, but there was no way to wash it.

I sat on the mattress and put on my well-worn shoes. I was then wearing all the clothes I owned, except my coat, which was too bulky to wear inside the sleeping bag. I pushed myself up with painful crackling in my knees. The cold air quickly wrapped around my shoulders and started sinking into me. I went to the reloading table, removed my coat from the back of the chair, and put it on.

With a hurried shuffle, I moved to the door and out, locking it with the key I always kept in my coat pocket. Then into a deeper cold, maybe low twenties, going down the stairs. I coughed involuntarily on the smoky sulfuric stink of last night's coal fires, belonging only to the privileged few. And the stench of everyone's raw sewage, from the many slit latrines in the complex. Funny, I thought, how only in raw sewage there is rare abundance, and even more rare equality among the residents of the compound.

It was only late November and I was already growing to hate the stink and the coal soot and the cold hunger of winter. I dreaded January and February. I walked down the sidewalk to the end of the building and pissed into the reeking slit latrine. It was too dark to see the muck in it, but the stench was surprising. I didn't think it could be so bad with the temperature so low. With my urge relieved, I paused and listened for signs of battle. But the pre-dawn darkness was as empty of sound as it was of light and warmth. The front was still near Williamsburg, according to the Block Leader's last propaganda announcements. But who knew? It had been a long time since I'd heard the distant artillery.

The ration truck was still parked between the first two buildings as I walked back toward the stairs.

I looked for the alien, but the truck sat by itself on the empty street. Only the truck's crew could be heard, moving rations and equipment between apartments in the building beside mine.

Hunger and worn knees slowed my climb up the steps. There was a time when I took steps two at a time, years before the war. Now, even with the steps one by one, the climb slowed with each flight of stairs. I needed more to eat, but I had nothing left beyond the daily rations. Even the thought of trying to kill a bird seemed as unlikely as sprinting up the street; virtually impossible. It had been a long time since I'd even seen a rat and all the cats and dogs were long gone. There was no black market any more, simply because we'd all been stripped of all possessions on entering the Blue zone.

Reentering the apartment, I felt its faint warmth. In theory, some heat was from the Building Leader's coal fire, down on the first floor. But it seemed very little heat came up from the lower floors. Mostly my body heat had warmed the place overnight, and I ached at the thought of even that energy expended.

I sat on my chair at the reloading table with my mouth hanging open, exhausted. Futile as it was, I couldn't help but wonder what the breakfast rations would be. There had often been rice or beans in the summer, but corn mush had become more common in the autumn. How I hated the stuff! The larger kernel pieces usually had centers as hard as gravel bits, because the mush was apparently boiled the very minimum amount of time. With the nearly constant mild scurvy causing my teeth to be sore, the corn mush was painful to chew. Nothing helped that; not chewing slowly and carefully, not leaving it to soak. Nothing.

There were also the little bits of meat, no matter what else the breakfast stew contained. The meat was fatty at first, then more and more lean. I decided not to think about the meat any longer.

I got up, shuffled to the pass-through opening between the now-useless kitchen and the empty space intended for a dining area. On the narrow countertop there, I kept the items required to be turned in at breakfast and dinner call, plus my wiped-clean metal bowl. In the morning, I turned in the used plastic sandwich bag, which had contained my bread ration, and two used plastic water bottles. The metal bowl would be presented for my breakfast stew.

I walked back to the chair at the reloading table, put the items on the table, and sat heavily. In a short time, I nodded off.

In my dream, a giant grasshopper alien and I were on a boat, and I had a paper bag full of sandwiches. In the bag, the sandwiches were small and cold. But when I opened one, it turned into a hot Reuben sandwich, complete with delicious-smelling corned beef, partly melted Swiss cheese, tangy sauerkraut, a thick Thousand Island dressing, all on thick slices of hot rye bread. I was telling the alien that these sandwiches were a special treat, but he refused to try one. Rather than eat, I persisted in trying to convince the alien to take a sandwich.

I awoke to a pounding on the door which sounded much more urgent than usual. I grabbed the plastic bag, the two bottles, and my bowl, then shuffled to the door quickly.

I opened it, and the Block Leader was right in the doorway.

"You don't want to eat? You don't want to work? What is this foolishness?"

"I'm sorry, Block Leader!"

The Block Leader turned to the Building Leader, off to the side, and shouted, "What are you running here? A vacation resort?"

"No, Block Leader! I assure you this Worker will be more attentive!"

The Block Leader turned back to me. "If you aren't ready, maybe I should send your ration back to the truck! Then you can sleep late!"

I cringed in horror.

"Please, Block Leader! I apologize for the delay! I'm ready to work, and I wish to welcome our special guest." I hoped that turning the conversation to the waiting alien would move things along. And then I saw it, standing behind the two ration bearers.

The Block Leader looked at me with disgust. "All right," he said. "Ration bearers, inside! Move your asses!"

The Block Leader and I moved aside, and the bearers entered. The alien followed them, wearing a segmented suit of metal and composite armor plates, carrying some kind of folded equipment. The alien's massive weight caused the apartment floor to creak in a way I hadn't heard before. It was tall and massive, yet its form was more humanoid than I had imagined. The Block Leader entered behind the alien. To the Building Leader, the Block Leader said, "Why don't you stay outside and busy yourself thinking up your usual excuses?!"

After he went out, I closed the door gently.

The alien looked around the apartment, but its attention soon focused on the reloading table. The bearers set the wooden box of reloading materials on the floor near the table and opened the ration container. I gave them the two empty bottles, got back two full of water, and swapped the empty bag for one with a slice of dark bread in it. Those I set down quickly and held out my bowl. In it, the ration server placed a measured scoop of soupy rice speckled with meat. I moved my rations onto the pass-through counter, and went back to the Block Leader.

He was watching me with a scowl. "Today, our honored guest here wishes to see your reloading process. Demonstrate and explain that process to our guest, carefully and completely! You will answer all his questions, but you may not ask him anything! Do you understand?"

"Yes, Block Leader!"

"I repeat, do NOT pose any questions to our honored guest!"

"Yes, Block Leader, I understand."

"I hope so! Our guest has a display screen, and you will read the questions from it carefully, then respond fully. The same device will translate your answers into their language. Is all this clear to you?"

"Yes, Block Leader!"

The Block Leader turned, opened the door, went out, and began shouting at the Building Leader. The ration bearers went out and I closed the door behind them. I was surprised the Block Leader had paid so little attention to the alien.

I turned to the alien, bowed—I'm not sure why—and said, "Welcome to my home."

The alien unfolded the object, and it became a strong-looking chair. It sat in the chair, pulled an overlay plate from the armor at the front of its rounded thorax, and held it up toward me. It was apparently the display screen. I shuffled over to read it.

In white letters on a blue-black background, it said, "Thank you for inviting me." The translator doesn't work very well, it seemed, because I had made no such invitation. Or maybe someone had told the alien that I had. So I'd better be careful how I interpret the text, I decided.

Without being turned or moved, the device display changed to: "Please, consume your morning meal and make any necessary preparations."

"Thank you."

The alien assumed what must have been a waiting pose, perfectly aligned on the chair, and apparently looking straight ahead at nothing. It remained motionless in that position.

I went to the counter, pulled my worn stainless-steel spoon from my upper coat pocket, and began eating the rice stew slowly while standing. I watched the motionless alien. Its massive form while standing somehow became even bigger while sitting, like a large hand transformed into an enormous fist. Maybe it was from a planet having stronger gravity. It was obviously wearing armor, but it was difficult to distinguish between the skin of the alien, its clothing—if there was any—and the armored outer suit.

The meat in the stew was lean, tough, and gristly. But the rice was still warm and delicious. And it was wonderful not having to chew corn mush again!

The alien's head, especially, was interesting. There was some kind of helmet plate and some kind of goggles over its large black eyes. The rest of its face was smooth, with small slanted holes all over its lower half, without a bulge for a nose. I couldn't determine whether it was wearing a face mask or not. The entire alien was a flat, medium-brown color overall, on both its metallic-looking and composite-looking surfaces. Was that its natural color, or was the color selected to serve as camouflage for duty on Earth? Its hands had a brown outer shell, segmented to allow movement, with small protruding barbs at the base of each knuckle. They looked cockroach-like, if cockroaches grew hands. Each hand had three claw/fingers and an opposing claw/thumb.

I couldn't help but speak to it, and maybe it was time to say something about reloading anyway. "I do not eat at the reloading table, to avoid contamination."

The alien did not move.

"I used to reload on this small pass-through counter, sitting on a high stool." The alien still didn't respond in any way, but I decided to continue anyway. "The light here wasn't very good, so far from the windows. So I asked for that table and chair. But when they brought those, they took my stool." Which I had hoped, becoming surplus, I could have traded for some food.

By then, the rice stew was gone, and the bowl licked almost clean. I had a drink from one of the water bottles, and replaced its cap. The bottle had the usual grime around its top, which I didn't want to think about. Instead, I examined the bread and the remaining water, which would be lunch, and found them to be of little interest. There was an alien sitting in the room, after all. So I reached through the pass-through opening, picked up one of the wiping rags from the kitchen counter, and wiped my bowl and spoon. The rag was getting filthy; it needed washing at the curb the next time it rained. I left the bowl on the pass-through counter and dropped the spoon into my upper coat pocket.

The alien was still motionless.

I said, "I need to go to the latrine again. I'll be back in a few minutes."

I went to the stinking latrine again, and then wiped the fingers of my left hand in the frost-covered grass until I could withstand the cold no longer. Back in the apartment, I found the alien in its same place, still motionless. I picked up the wooden reloading supplies box they'd left for me, moved it closer to the table, and sat in my chair. I was surprised to see less than the usual allocation.

"Today I've been issued only 100 small pistol primers. Usually there are 200. Maybe there are fewer so I can spend more time explaining the process." As I said that, I wasn't sure I believed it. But why else? Making my 200-round quota of 9mm ammunition had always been of critical importance and non-negotiable. I continued to empty the box, placing and arranging materials on the table.

"There is a bag of cast lead bullets, probably 100 of them, maybe a few more, said to weigh 125 grains each. And the canister of powder I've been using lately, and a bag of used 9mm cartridge cases."

I looked through the bag of empty cases and there didn't seem to be any blood on them. So I went into the kitchen to fetch a wiping rag reserved for reloading, leaving it dry. I used a wet rag to wipe off blood, but I saved the water whenever I could.

I sat at the table, arranged everything, and looked at the alien. It still stared into nothingness. I said, "I'm ready to begin, and I seem to have all the necessary materials available."

With that, the alien got up, repositioned its chair opposite mine at the table, and sat again. It again popped the display panel from the indented frame in its chest armor, and held it toward me.

The display read: "Please proceed. I am very interested in your metallic cartridge technology." I wondered why, but I remembered not to ask. The display changed to: "We are students of military history and all military technologies."

Great, I thought. This is some kind of living history lesson, in what—for them—must be an obscure and antique technology. Fine. I'd long felt like a used-up antique anyway.

"I begin by wiping the outside of each case and checking the interior for contamination. If any dirt or blood is visible inside a case, I wipe in there too. For each operation, I place the cases in progress into this plastic reloading block. It holds fifty cases." I began inspecting and wiping the cases, gradually filling the fifty holes in the reloading block.

The alien followed my work with its display panel, as though it was recording a video. At one point, it held the display up, closer to my face. The display read: "Are other methods used to clean cases?"

"Yes. A favorite of mine was walnut hull cleaning media, in a vibratory cleaning machine. I've used tumbling cleaning machines too. Those methods were efficient for all kinds of dry dust and dirt and polished the brass cases. I really liked all that polished brass, too. But I no longer have those devices." They, like so much else, had been left in Covington.

The panel changed again, now displaying: "What metals are used to make the cases?"

"Cases have been made from various metals in the past. Steel and aluminum were used for inexpensive, disposable cases. Brass was more expensive, but it was the best material, and brass cases are reloadable. I'm not sure, but I think production of new ammunition ceased a few years ago. So only these used, reloadable brass cases remain in use."

"What alloy of brass are these cases?"

"I don't know the proportions. But I believe they are a mixture of copper and zinc." The alien moved the panel from the "read this" position back to the "making a video" position, so I resumed work.

Finally, I had fifty wiped and inspected cases in the reloading block. I opened the bag of bullets and took one out. I showed the alien that the bullet would drop into an empty casing.

"When fired, the brass cartridge case expands to the firearm's chamber walls, then contracts slightly as the firing pressure subsides. The case is left slightly oversized and too big to grip a new bullet. So the cases need to be formed back to their initial diameter using a reloading press and a carbide sizing die. The advantage of the carbide die is that it does not require lubrication of the case. The sizing die also has a decapping pin, which pushes the old primer out of the case."

I took the hand reloading press from its worn-fuzzy cardboard box and opened the plastic reloading die box. I held up the pieces I was about to use for the alien. As I expected, the alien held its display panel up to each one. Then I snapped the shell holder into the reloading die ram and fitted the carbide sizing die into the top of the press.

"The rim at the base of a used cartridge case is held in the shell holder, like this. Then, when I squeeze the handle of the hand press, the ram pushes the case up into the die, like this."

I squeezed the case into the die, and I heard the old primer pop out. I then pulled the handle open, to pull the case out of the die. Dropping the reloading press into my lap, I held up the sized case and the bullet I'd used before. I showed that the bullet would no longer fit into the case. And I turned the head of the case toward the alien, so it could see and record the empty primer pocket.

The panel display changed again and asked: "What is the source of the bullets?"

"I'm not sure. The bullets sometimes arrive still warm. Maybe another Worker nearby is making them, with a casting furnace to melt lead and a bullet mold. Maybe with lead from old car batteries or recovered bullets. I'm not sure. I used factory-made, copper-jacketed bullets for a time, but those ran out."

I put the case into the reloading block and held up the reloading press. "The shell holder has a hole in it." I snapped the shell holder from the ram, to demonstrate. "And the ram is hollow. About twenty-five of the old small pistol primers will fit into it before it needs to be emptied."

The alien held up its display to me again. It read: "Please explain how 'small pistol' relates to the primers."

"Primers are small or large by their overall diameter, as required by the size of the brass case. And they are made for either pistol or rifle cartridges. The rifle primers, both small and large diameter, have more explosive material to ignite the larger quantity of gunpowder in the bigger rifle cartridges. Nine millimeter pistol cases need the smaller diameter primers, so the correct primer type for them is 'small pistol.'"

I put everything back together and began sizing and decapping the other forty-nine cases in the reloading block. The alien didn't seem to have any interest in handling anything and I couldn't ask if it wanted to. So I kept working. After twenty-five cases, I slipped off the die and shell holder, then dumped the old primers from the hollow ram into a waste can I kept under the table.

"May I see the discarded primers?"

"Certainly."

I picked up the can and held it toward the alien. The alien scanned it with the display device, but didn't seem interested in taking any primers from the can. So I picked an old primer from the can, held it in my right palm, and turned it with my left index finger as he recorded it closely. That done, I dropped the primer back into the can and went back to work. Soon I emptied the second set of twenty-five used primers from the ram.

With the first fifty cases sized and decapped, I set the reloading press aside. I then picked up one of the cases, pointed the head of the case toward the alien, and showed it the empty primer pocket.

"The primer pockets still contain burned residue from the old primers. If it's not removed, ignition could be affected. So I use this tool, a primer pocket cleaner, to clean them."

I began giving each of the fifty primer pockets a couple of twists with the tool, then tapping the head of the given case on the table. Each left a trace of black powdery residue. Again, I did all fifty. As always, I felt pain in my wrist and elbow with each twist of the primer pocket cleaning tool. But ergonomics and repetitive-motion injuries no longer mattered.

My aches and pains prompted thoughts of better times. "I used to clean the primer pockets so much better," I said, my mind wandering.

The alien's display read: "How has your process changed, and why?"

"I used to scrape out the primer pockets with this cross-blade tool, being turned by an electric drill motor. Then I would more carefully scrape them again with the sharpened end of a bamboo chopstick. I also used the sharpened end to clean all residue from the flash hole, the hole between the primer pocket and the interior of the case. Then I would clean the primer pockets with cotton swabs wet with isopropyl alcohol, to be sure no contaminants would affect the primers."

I had to explain what a bamboo chopstick was, and then describe the cleaning and degreasing with cotton swabs.

The alien's display panel asked: "If all that was necessary, why not perform those cleaning operations now?"

I sighed. "Maybe it wasn't necessary. Not for ammunition used as soon as these cartridges will be. It was pride in craftsmanship, mostly. Also, my ammunition was sometimes not fired for years, and I wanted to protect the primers from any form of contamination. Even oily skin residues can degrade the primer material. So I even wiped my fingertips on a paper towel damp with alcohol, before I picked up each primer. Clearly, all that was an obsession with making perfect ammunition, and maybe not needed at a practical level. I never had a cartridge misfire, in all the years I reloaded, and I took great satisfaction in that. But now, it's different. Tools and materials are limited, and time is even more limited, with a production quota to meet."

"It is interesting that reloading for military use is to a lower standard."

"It is. That reminds me of Orwell, George Orwell, describing the sub-standard reloads in *Homage to Catalonia*, his memoir of the Spanish Civil War. But yes, military arms production has often been sub-standard. Our history is full of production allocated to the lowest bidder, production workers hurrying to make quota, and hastily built or hastily repaired armaments production plants." And starving, exhausted slave laborers, I thought. But I was already tired of complaining to the alien.

"I know of the philosopher George Orwell. His writings form the basis of your systems of government, it seems."

The alien's statement stunned me for a moment. I began to contradict him, but it seemed futile.

"Have there been any misfires with the ammunition you have produced here?"

"Uh, not that I know of."

I didn't want to imagine how a dissatisfied customer's experience would be conveyed back to me. I was sure it wouldn't be pleasant. My stomach knotted at the thought of it. It was certainly time to refocus on my work.

"Next, new primers are installed." I took an old piece of aluminum foil from my kit, and flattened it slightly on the table, letting the edges stay slightly raised. I then emptied half of the box of 100 primers onto the aluminum foil, by sliding the cover only halfway off their inverted plastic tray. "Primers are sensitive to static electricity discharges, so I handle them on metal. This wrinkled aluminum foil also provides a surface to keep them from rolling away."

The sizing die was already removed from the press, to dump old primers, so I installed the priming adapter where it had been. I unsnapped the shell holder from the ram and slipped it into the priming adapter. I then snapped the primer pusher assembly into the ram. "Now, the case is held at the top of the press, and a primer will be pressed into the base of each one."

I squeezed the press until the primer pusher extended through the shell holder, and showed the alien. Then I took a primer, placed it into the pusher, retracted it below the shell holder, placed a case into the shell holder, and squeezed the press gently. I released it, removed the case, and showed the alien that the case contained a new primer.

"Primers must be pressed at least flush into the head of the case. Otherwise, the bolt or slide of the weapon will strike the primer as the cartridge is chambered, and the cartridge could fire prematurely."

Again, I processed the other forty-nine cases.

"Next, the expander die is used to open the mouth of each case just enough to accept a bullet."

I removed the primer tools, put the shell holder back into the ram, and installed the second die into the press. Again, I showed the alien that a bullet wouldn't fit into a sized case. Then I pressed the case into the expander die and showed how the case mouth was flared slightly. I then demonstrated how the base of a bullet would go part way into the case, and even stick there, from friction.

Again, the other forty-nine. But I was tiring.

"I have to take a break." I got up and walked around the apartment a while. I wanted some bread, but it was still far too early. So I had only a sip of water.

I stretched and sat down at the table again.

There was the device again, with "The reloading dies seem to be threaded along their entire length for adjustments. How are they adjusted?" displayed on its screen.

I opened the reloading die box, and pulled the folded instruction sheet from the lid. I unfolded it, placed it on the table, and said, "Would you . . . I mean, please scan this sheet for complete instructions." The alien scanned the full sheet carefully, front and back.

"Next, gunpowder is added to the cases. But first, I need to show you how the appropriate amount is determined." I picked up my old reloading manual, and opened it to the bookmarked 9mm section. "In the manual, this powder is shown as having a starting charge of 3.3 grains, and maximum of 3.6 grains." I replaced the manual and pulled out the yellowed paperboard slide calculator for the powder dippers. "This paper calculator shows there is a dipper available within this range. The 0.5cc dipper holds 3.5 grains; so, being within the range, it's an acceptable powder charge."

I opened the powder canister and poured powder into my one-cup metal measuring cup until it was about three-quarters full. I then picked the 0.5cc plastic dipper from the dipper set and scooped powder from the cup and dumped it back several times. When the powder was releasing well, with no adhesion to the scoop, I made a well-practiced scoop for measure. I picked up a piece of index card with a straight edge and carefully scraped the excess powder from the top of the dipper. Dropping the piece of index card, I next picked up the powder funnel and placed the funnel over one of the cases. I then dumped the powder into the funnel and tapped the dipper against the inside of the funnel. Carefully, I took it from the reloading block and held it up for the alien to see.

Again, the other forty-nine cases were processed.

Then I carefully moved the reloading block toward the window, catching some oblique sunlight, and tipped the block slightly. "Now, I compare the amount of powder in each case to check for mistakes. Sometimes a case is found to have no powder, or a double charge. But all these appear to have the same amount of powder, so they're good.

"Next, a bullet goes into each case. If the expander die is adjusted properly, the bullet base will jam slightly into the mouth of the case."

I placed bullets into the cases, slightly pressing each bullet into place as vertically as possible. Each one stuck slightly into place.

"Next, I place the seating die into the press, like this. Now, I place each case into the shell holder, being careful not to tip the bullet out, like so." I squeezed the reloading press handle, then pulled the cartridge from the die. I held it toward the alien. "A finished cartridge."

Still, the alien wouldn't touch the offered part.

"Since I'm not able to measure the cartridge's overall length with these lead bullets, I've left the bullet seating die at the same setting as the jacketed bullets and the result seems satisfactory. I just check that the bullets appear to be seated consistently. That's with the die itself still set for the proper taper crimp, so the case mouth grips the bullet tightly."

Once more, I processed the other forty-nine cases.

"Sometimes, a fourth die is used to crimp and post-size the cartridges. I have one here." I held it up.

"But it was decided that I should not use it, to allow more cartridges to be processed per day. That was intended as a wartime emergency measure."

I moved the fifty cartridges from the reloading block to a plastic ammo box tray, then placed it into the worn paperboard ammo box as it came from the original manufacturer.

I stood and stretched my aching arms. My right elbow was especially sore. Considering my wording carefully, I said "If you have no further questions, I will take my mid-day break."

The alien held its display to me, which read, "Before your break, please describe how you came to accumulate in-depth knowledge of this technology."

"Books, at first. I read how-to guides first, then the books having loading data for all the cartridges. Then the instructions which come with the reloading equipment. Those were most important, because they described the adjustment and use of the reloading dies. Finally, I built experience while reloading tens of thousands of rounds. I have not had any formal instruction on reloading, as in a classroom."

"I congratulate you on mastering this technology, as you have surely done."

"Thank you."

"Please, rest and take nourishment according to your schedule."

✦ ✦ ✦

After the heavy bread, which included both the taste and texture of sawdust, I finished the first bottle of water. My lunch break was earlier than usual, after reloading only fifty rounds, so I had taken extra time to eat the horrible bread even more slowly than usual. That was beneficial, to better feel for the inedible chunks always present in the bread. Some seemed to be bits of wood, others bits of stone.

During my entire break, the alien sat still again. I wondered whether it was so highly disciplined, or simply a machine which could be placed into a standby mode. Probably the former, I thought. Its enthusiasm for learning about reloading seemed excessive for a machine.

While reloading the remaining fifty rounds, the alien was just as attentive and interested as during the first fifty. When I had finished, rearranged my equipment, and packed everything into the wooden reloading materials box, the alien held the display to me again. It read, "I have sent a message stating that I have completed my visit. Thank you."

"Thank you for visiting my home. I hope the information I have presented is helpful."

I heard a heavy truck arrive at the front of the building. That was unusual. It was too early for the dinner ration, so I carried the wooden box to the door while the alien folded its chair. I hesitated, not knowing whether to open the door or not. Finally, I did, just in time to see the Block Leader at the top of the stairs, followed by heavily-armed Blue Guards.

"Good afternoon, asshole!" said the Block Leader in a mocking voice, pretending to be cheerful.

"Please come in," I replied meekly. He did, while I held the door. The first of the Blue Guards pushed me back into the apartment, the third closed the door behind him.

"There are no more primers," the Block Leader said with a smirk. "The ones you used today were the last 100. So you have been declared excess. We won't need your expertise for machetes."

My throat tightened. I noticed the alien raising its display panel, and turned to read it.

It showed: "Please read this aloud."

So I did. Soon it changed to read: "This worker was very cooperative and I thank you all for this informative demonstration." Then: "I hope that you enjoyed your career. It must have been pleasant to work with this metallic cartridge technology."

"Ha!" laughed the Block Leader. "I hope you'll enjoy being in my rice tomorrow morning, you skinny bastard. It better not taste as bad as you smell!"

My focus remained on the alien and my temper flared.

"No, I didn't enjoy this, this life of hunger and suffering!" I wanted to say more, to explain all that had been taken from me, the pain of my horrid existence, and now the sudden loss of all hope. But the right words eluded me, and I just felt exhausted. I wasn't even sure I cared anymore.

The Block Leader raised his hand. At first I thought it was for silence, but then I noticed one of the Blue Guards had a carbine butt raised and aimed at my head.

The alien held up the display again, but I read only to myself: "We researched your history carefully. You lived as your people have always lived. We made sure that your lives would not be changed in the least when we took control."

The Block Leader's hand dropped, and the carbine butt slammed into the left side of my head, knocking me to my knees. I was hustled from the apartment and I was strangely relieved to be rid of it.

"Goodbye, shitty life!" I mumbled.

Roughly, I was loaded into the truck, and two of the Blue Guards sat and watched me with little interest as the truck lurched into motion. The ride was noisy and bouncy, but I knew it would be short.

The alien was right, I thought. This was how we had always lived, especially during the many wars, the many sieges, through countless years of hunger and privation since the dawn of time. Only the particulars of various weapon technologies had changed. The aliens were right to continue our natural way of life. It was what we'd always known, what we'd always had, and what we'd always deserved. But I'd hoped that someday we could rise above our misery and finally change our situation for the better. Would the aliens help us or would they instead choose to maintain the status quo? Maybe I'd already heard the answer.

So finally, I could only hope to die by the product of my own work and not by the machetes.

THE CONFESSION

What are humans? What makes us who we are, especially as explorers and conquerors of Planet Earth?

Does our present existence on this now-subdued planet mask our true nature? If so, what would we be if we were somehow separated from this too-familiar setting?

I suspect Michael Shaara's insightful All the Way Back *contains answers to questions we're usually not willing to ask of ourselves. So I thought of those kinds of questions while writing this story. And these:*

If it were stripped down to the bare essentials and the inescapable cold realities—economics, especially—what would an invasion of Earth be like?

Who would the invaders be?

After the high-value targets were inevitably destroyed in the opening rounds, who would remain as the defenders of Earth?

This is Investigator Harris, Afton County Sheriff's Department, Bridgeport, Virginia. The time is 7:56 PM. Subject being interviewed has refused to identify himself. He's our eighth John Doe, so for the record he'll be called John Doe 8 until such time as he identifies himself.

IH: Where did you come from?

JD8: Here, from this planet, of course. We were taught it took years to gather the reproductive tissue samples. Maybe two hundred eggs from each girl who was abducted and a few thousand sperm from each boy. Those were combined in the scout ships, using a process that had been refined for gender yield. The few female embryos were discarded, then the males were preserved until they could be gestated.

IH: How long did that process take?

JD8: Who knows? Thousands of years, at least.

IH: Where were you and all the others, between collection of those samples and your arrival back on Earth?

JD8: I have no idea. Again, I know only from our classes that we were gestated and incubated within facilities on the transports which also carried our assault ships here. But I have no recollection of that. As early as I can remember, I lived in my assault ship in the holding cells for my light infantry platoon.

IH: Describe how you came of age.

JD8: A significant day comes to mind. We were little taller than Feld's waist when he killed the first of us—

IH: Who is Feld?

JD8: A platoon sergeant, you would say. We were in our usual morning formation, with our places determined by our boyish aggressiveness, from the most dominant first to the most docile last. Our competition for ranking had been little more than pushing and horseplay up to that point, but that first boy's death marked the end of our play.

The formation began with Feld blowing his whistle, the same as always. We ran naked from our crowded cells to our familiar places in two lines, facing each other. My low ranking meant I had to run across the hallway to my place near the inner surface of the ship's hull. The boy who would be killed that morning stood beside me.

"Attention!" Feld shouted, but we were already motionless, standing stiffly at the position of attention. He walked between our two rows, inspecting us calmly.

"Good morning, soldiers!"

"Good morning, Feld!" we all shouted as loudly as we could.

"Before breakfast, you should consider your ranking. Your ranking is very important and will determine how you move forward. Do any of you wish to challenge your ranking this morning?"

We were silent and no one moved.

"Good!" he said, passing in front of me. He was pulling his sidearm from his holster, but I didn't yet understand the purpose or effect of a sidearm.

"Then as you will soon see, there will be four results."

He leveled his sidearm at the lowest-ranking boy beside me, and shot him between his eyes. I jumped at the sound of the shot; more than the others, I'm sure.

"Attention!" Feld shouted, and we quickly resumed our proper positions. At that time, we had no way of understanding a shot from a sidearm is the least-noisy sound of battle.

"First is the bullet," he said. "Second is the cartridge casing." He poked my chest with his sidearm. "You! Find them both. The bullet will be a mashed piece of gray metal. The casing will be a small cylinder, closed on one end."

I turned to where the boy had been standing, and I froze at the sight of his blood and the bits of brain on the hull, all surrounding a circular, metallic impact point.

"Look for them on the floor, idiot!" Feld screamed in my right ear. I dropped to my knees and began searching. Feld was returning his sidearm to his holster.

"Third is meat for your soup after class today, thanks to this boy with no ambition, and no martial spirit. You and you, take the remains to the kitchen!"

The next two boys beside my place in formation jumped to the dead boy, and began lifting him. Then one of them vomited onto the dead boy's ruined head.

"Pig!" Feld shouted, and kicked him. "You think the others want your mess on their stew meat?"

I found the cartridge case right away. At the time, I marveled at how warm it felt in my hand while I was looking for the bullet.

"The fourth and final result is that, from today, you will understand the importance of your ranking!"

I knew I was then the lowest-ranking boy, but I resolved to advance, and quickly. I saw the bullet after the dead boy was carried away, in the pool of his blood. I picked it up and stood, looking at it. I ignored the blood; I was amazed that metal could be flattened so much by its impact on the hull wall. At that time, I didn't know about the relative hardness of metals.

Feld's slap brought my study of the bullet to a sudden end. "Take those to the armory, now! Like your friend, nothing goes to waste!

"The rest of you, wash and get into your uniforms. Breakfast in ten minutes!"

And so our long day began.

IH: Before we go any further, what was done with that boy's body?

JD8: That night, our soup was delicious! I'd never had meat before or tasted the broth it makes with water. So maybe you know what to do with me!

IH: Very funny. What was your food when there was no meat?

JD8: A thick soup, twice a day. It was mealy and bland, usually. We were told it was made with enriched synthetic grain, but we knew nothing of real grain. The food here is much better.

IH: So the day that boy was killed was significant in your coming of age?

JD8: Yes, it was, in several ways. It was the first day of our more structured classes. Maybe the same as beginning the first year in your elementary schools.

We also began a new level in our military studies. The front armor plate I was wearing when I was captured was issued to me that day. But then, I held it with my left forearm, as a heavy shield. If you care to, check its inside surface. It still has the mounting holes for the hand grip and forearm loop I used then. Along with my shield, I was issued my first weapon, a polymer practice gladius.

Also—

IH: Excuse me. What's a gladius?

JD8: A short sword, used primarily by the ancient Romans on your world. Ours were plastic at that time, with dull edges and a blunted end. But we learned much while training with them.

IH: Thank you. Please continue.

JD8: That day, we learned that our place in the platoon had to be earned. More than that, we were told—and shown—that only earning a place in the platoon would keep us alive. The numbers were quite simple; there were only twenty-four places.

IH: I don't understand. Please elaborate.

JD8: We had been living in six small cells, six of us in each cell, with a three-high bunk bed mounted to each side wall. Later, we were shown how our bunks would be converted to high-G restraints for landing. But two of the cells had to be emptied. One was needed to stow weapons for landing and provide a high-G restraint for Feld.

The sixth cell was needed for ammunition and stores for immediate issue and use after landing. Until then, ammunition had to be stowed separately from weapons at all times, in the Legion storerooms.

So initially twelve boys were excess, and they eventually lost their places. Two were lost during live-fire exercises, the rest to ranking selection. We were taught that competition would make us better and make our platoons better. But our weight was the real limit, an absolute limit. The ship's maximum landing weight was critical for atmospheric entry, glide, and landing performance. And the maximum landing weight was planned for the average weight of the twenty-four soldiers, plus the platoon sergeant, for forty platoons. I did not see their quarters, but we were taught that an additional sixty-four places were reserved for the Centurions, two cooks and an armorer per Century, the Tribune and his staff, and the ship's crew. So there were 1,064 total places per ship. No extra weight was allowed, and any excess items were consumed or jettisoned before landing.

IH: What about instructors for your classes?

JD8: Those were taught mostly by our Centurion or our armorer, and some were taught by members

	of the Tribune's staff. A few, in classes relating to ship's functions, were taught by the ship's crew.
IH:	Where did the leadership and support staff come from?
JD8:	Here, the same as us. But they were gestated in the vats years before we were, then developed and trained for their positions. The Tribune and his staff are twenty years older than I am. The assault ship's crew and our Centurions are fifteen years older, the rest of the cadre are ten years older. Like us, their positions were determined competitively.
IH:	What was your training like, generally?
JD8:	Basic and simple, at first. We have always spoken your language; since infancy, I suppose. But the language classes which began that first day of formal training were for learning to read and write. Those classes were always the first of the morning. Your history was the second class—
IH:	Before that, what were you told about why you were learning our language?
JD8:	We were taught this language because it was the one spoken in our ship's target area. With the same physical appearance, speaking the language would allow us to be used for special missions within areas still under your control.

IH: Have you performed such missions?

JD8: Yes, I was ordered to Charlottesville to gather information on public sentiment, condition of approach routes and roads, and possible targets for the demolition bombs.

IH: Did you report that kind of information and do you know whether that information was used?

JD8: Yes. I walked out of the city, east on Route 250 at first, and then went cross-country. I rejoined our forces near Barboursville. I was debriefed immediately and I made a full report. I'd like to think my information was helpful in taking Charlottesville the following week.

IH: How did you get through our lines, into and out of Charlottesville?

JD8: Getting in was easy, with the tide of refugees moving south. I rode south on Route 29 on a flatbed truck, with more than 100 refugees. Getting out was more difficult. I walked east on 250 to a mountain on the left, then went to higher ground. I expected to be able to move without being seen in the wooded mountains, and I believed your defensive positions would be fewer and weaker than along the roads. Those assumptions turned out to be correct. Your defensive positions on the mountain were

	poorly arranged and did not have sufficient visibility to each other, so I was able to advance to an isolated position and neutralize it.
IH:	Tell me how you were able to do that and what became of the people in that position.
JD8:	The position was along the top of the mountain, just past an intersection at the end of a road. It was raining, and I made almost no noise walking on the road very slowly. We were trained to step at an irregular pace, to avoid making any recognizable pattern of sounds.
	As I advanced to the position, I could see only one guard was awake; he was facing the opposite direction, toward the top of the wooded ridgeline. He wasn't holding his weapon; his hands were under his poncho and he was barely awake. As I approached, I saw his helmet lying at his side. So I picked it up and hit him with it. He heard my final step behind him, but it was too late. The other guard was awakened when he fell, but I was able to use the helmet on him too.
IH:	What was the condition of the guards when you left them?
JD8:	Dead and disarmed. I took an armored vest from one of the bodies, which was about my size. Then I collected as much ammunition as

	I could carry, some food and a canteen, and both weapons, which were M4 carbines. I then walked along the top of the ridgeline to the northeast. I carried one M4 and had the other slung over my back.
IH:	Do you realize the seriousness of your actions?
JD8:	I am a Soldier, and I'm serious in everything I do. And I am not ashamed of anything I've done. So I'll tell you my story the same as I would tell anyone in my platoon.
IH:	Then why have you refused to identify yourself to us?
JD8:	My identity isn't important. You may call me "Soldier."
IH:	So were you and your fellow soldiers wearing uniforms during your initial landing?
JD8:	Yes.
IH:	Did you wear your uniform during your Charlottesville operation?
JD8:	No, I was disguised as a refugee.
IH:	Yes, that's what I thought. But for a more complete record, please describe your travels before you arrived in Charlottesville, and then we'll talk more about your movements after your departure.

JD8:   My assault ship was assigned to conduct the assault on Reagan National Airport. Have you seen any of our ships?

IH: No.

JD8:   They're simple lifting-body designs, with a vertical fin on each side. In the transports, they were stacked three high, and the stacks fit closely together, with the stacks alternately pointing inboard and outboard. They have massively thick nickel-steel hulls, with a thin ceramic coating on their noses, bottoms, and vertical fins. Although they're heavier than any of your vehicles, they're simple, and they must have been easy to mass produce. They have no drive engines, only maneuvering thrusters, and no landing gear. There are two electrical generators which power everything in the ship, from life support to flight controls. After landing, the assault units exit through jettisonable doors, which have explosive bolts. Obviously, the ships are used just once.

The ships can be landed onto any flat surface. They can touch down on water and skim across the water to decelerate before beaching. Ours was landed on the Potomac River. It touched down just north of the Wilson Bridge, with a planned beaching onto runway 1 on the airport. But one of the deep-penetration demolition bombs used to destroy Washington was late to detonate. When it finally went off, the shock wave caused our ship to veer left. So after coming ashore, it crashed through a parking lot and into the terminal building. The riverbank and the base of the building gave us a rough ride, but the high-G restraints worked perfectly. We were out of them in seconds, to weapons and ammunition issue, and out of the ship within a minute.

For our objective, crashing into the terminal building might have been better than the original plan. When the exit doors were blown, the building debris was cleared away enough for us to egress, and we quickly secured the airport. One of the other ships was crashed into your Pentagon building intentionally, so the ships were known to be good for that kind of attack.

From there, my century moved south and west. We fought in the major battle at Manassas, and we were in Culpepper when I was assigned my mission to Charlottesville.

IH: And you said you re-joined your century in Barboursville?

JD8: Yes. I was re-armed and re-equipped. But getting deloused and cleaned up was the best. Your planet is filthy!

IH: That's how we like it. Where did you proceed from there?

JD8: We moved toward Charlottesville. My century was one of three to protect our right flank during the attack through the ruins. There were two centuries of light infantry and another with heavy weapons.

We advanced to the base of Lewis Mountain without any apparent resistance. We were to support the century with laser cannons, who were to take up positions at the top. But going up the mountain, the vehicle I was driving was blown up. I don't know how that happened. I regained consciousness after I had been captured, and was being evacuated for medical treatment. And then, I assume, I was brought to this detention facility.

IH: That's true. Please state your injuries, for the record.

JD8: I've had a concussion, and the left side of my head is heavily bruised. My left arm was broken.

IH: Also for the record: have your wounds been treated?

JD8: Yes, my arm has been set, and the cast is comfortable. But it's starting to itch. I've been told that no treatment exists for my concussion at this time.

IH: This is important. Who are you doing this for?

JD8: I could say my platoon, and Feld. We grew up preparing to fight together and we've fought well. But I'll assume instead that you mean The Masters.

IH: Who are The Masters?

JD8: I can tell you all about myself, my unit, and all we've done. The Masters won't care about any of that. None of us, and none of you, are of any concern to them. They want this planet seized, probably to mine iron and other heavy metals from it, and so it will be. I was told that's all they care about.

Otherwise, we were taught very little about them, not even the real name of their race. They created us, the perfect soldiers for this battle, and they gave us our mission. That's all we are, all we need, and all we will ever be.

Even if you were able to beat us, which you won't, you can't know who The Masters really are. You can't counterattack their world. You'll never even find it.

IH: I see. Love a happy ending. Do you have a closing statement?

JD8:   No. I've said enough. Get on with it.

The next morning, well before sunrise, Investigator Harris was awakened by someone's office door slamming. Which didn't make sense at first, because he'd been dreaming he was sleeping in a forest as a refugee. He rolled out of the sleeping bag on his office floor, groaned, and paused on all fours. He was sore and stiff. Slowly, he stood and switched on his desk lamp, by force of habit. But of course, there was no electricity.

He found his flashlight, then finally found some clean socks and underwear in a plastic trash bag. He'd have to wear his stale polyester uniform another day, but at least he didn't have to worry about food stains on it. With his just-as-stale towel around his waist, he grabbed his toiletry kit from his desk and went to the men's room to clean up. Hopefully, there would still be water.

After returning to his office, he put on his uniform, brown western boots, and his gun belt. He was already accustomed to the uniform again, after wearing civilian clothes for almost ten years. But civilian clothes weren't an option after the invasion. He straightened up his office quickly and went to the common area between the offices. There was some coffee, but nothing to eat. He poured some coffee into a brown waxed-paper cup, and walked to the sheriff's office. May as well get this day rolling, he thought.

He sipped some coffee, cleared his throat, and knocked on the closed door.

"Come!" shouted Sheriff Jacobs.

Harris opened the door, and saw the sheriff was cleaning his M16 by the light of an LED lantern on a corner of his desk. "Morning, Sheriff. Read my report?"

"Yes, thank you," said the sheriff, nodding toward it. Harris saw his report on top of the sheriff's cluttered desk.

"I'm sorry there's nothing to eat this morning. I've requested supplies from both the state police and the county, but times are tough."

"I'm OK."

"Also, I know I asked you to interview that boy and to write up a full report. But I regret that. It was a waste of time."

"Why?"

"It's obvious, isn't it? We're getting whipped, and it damn well might be the end of us if they make a push toward Staunton."

"Yeah, I know."

"Harris, I'll send up your report. Maybe it has something usable in it, maybe not. That's not for me to figure out anyway. It could end up being leaked to the press—the remnants of those jackals, anyway—and then become a real morale killer. People won't want to hear what we're really up against. Things are bad enough as they are."

Sheriff Jacobs turned in his swivel chair, with the upper receiver of his M16 still across his lap, and looked out his window. "It's a hell of a thing, using our own against us. But it's smart. They seem to have made as many people as they need. All they need to do is grow 'em in vats, smack 'em around some, and then fill 'em full of our own military history. Our military heritage apparently became their way of life."

"I still think it's weird how well he speaks English," said Harris.

"Nothing weird about that. In between re-enacting every battle in Earth's history, they were probably shown all the television programs we've ever transmitted. Imagine that, everything from *Leave It to Beaver* to the Kardashians."

"Ha! I bet that worked wonders for motivation!"

"No doubt," agreed Jacobs, without any sign of humor. The sheriff rocked backward in his swivel chair, and continued, now looking at Harris. "That's the hell of it. They're the same as us, the same as we've always been;

ready to kill whoever they're told to kill. Programmable as a damned computer."

"Yeah," said Harris. "And they're perfectly adapted to operate here on Earth, of course. There's no need for three-legged alien infantry wearing bulky Earth suits. They're able to pass as any one of us, and probably cheaper to make than robots."

"Yep, certainly, if you want to minimize the equipment involved and you know you'll have so many years of space travel. There'd be all the time you'd need for any kind of biology project, and then some. Those sons of bitches—" The sheriff turned in his chair to the window again. "What do you think of his statement, as it relates to the decree of martial law?"

"There are multiple capital offenses; take your pick. An operation behind our lines while not in his uniform, killing at least two of our people during all that, spying, seizing military weapons, goodness knows what else."

"Yes, there's no doubt," replied the sheriff, still looking out the window. "Well, you know the decree. Pick two deputies; take him out back and shoot him."

"Yes, Sheriff. I'll go do it now."

Deputies Persinger and Vass entered the cell and handcuffed John Doe 8's arms behind his back. They were careful with his cast, and used a second pair of cuffs as an extension, to avoid pulling too tightly against his left wrist.

"I apologize for not offering breakfast. There are food shortages now," said Investigator Harris.

"Wow, I'm sorry for your tough luck," said John Doe 8 with a smile.

The deputies led him from his cell, through the still-dark processing area, and into the hallway toward the back door.

"I'll assume I'm not being released on my own recognizance," John Doe 8 quipped.

"No, you're not," said Harris, opening the back door and holding it for the others. "We've got just one thing more for you."

"That's what I thought."

Once outside, the two deputies led the prisoner toward an old utility pole, which seemed to have been in the back alley forever. Deputy Persinger took out another pair of handcuffs and attached the prisoner's right arm to one of the telephone pole's galvanized steel guy wires. He then walked to the others.

"Take your places," said Harris.

Vass nodded, without looking up. The two deputies faced the prisoner, side by side, about ten yards away.

"I have a request," said John Doe 8. He was squinting while looking at them, toward the brightening sky. For just an instant, he looked like an innocent young boy who'd lost his glasses.

"What is it?" asked Harris.

"Do you remember the boy I told you about, the first one killed by Feld?"

"Yes."

"For him, it was quick and easy. I would prefer to go out that way."

"Sure," said Harris. He walked to the boy, pulling his .40 auto from its holster. Once he stood facing the boy, he paused and sighed. Then he lifted the pistol and fired it into the boy's forehead, almost in one motion.

The boy twisted and fell, with the handcuff quickly sliding down the guy wire. The boy's legs twitched for a short time, and then he was still.

"Leave him," said Harris, still looking down at the boy. "His people will be here soon enough. Like this, they will see how he died."

"Why is that important?" asked Vass.

"Who cares?" said Persinger.

"They'll know he was a Soldier to the end, and he must have done something to really piss off the enemy. They'll see honor in that." Harris turned to the two deputies. "Now go get ready. We'll be seeing more of them today or tomorrow. A lot more of them than there are of us."

With that, they walked back toward the building's back door. Harris stopped short.

Persinger stopped and looked back. "What's up?" he asked.

"Go ahead and get geared up," said Harris. "I'm going to stay here for this sunrise. Alone."

"He's always been a nature boy," said Persinger to Vass, who giggled. The deputies went inside.

The eastern horizon, heightened by the Blue Ridge Mountains, was brightening from a glaring, reddish orange to a brilliant yellow. Harris thought it was odd, seemingly a sunset in reverse. But it was beautiful, even if it felt more like an ending than a beginning.

"Not bad for this old ball of scrap iron," Harris said to himself, walking toward the back door. Then he wondered what the new owners would make of the Earth, after it had been recycled.

ETERNAL WAR

The next story describes my sin.

I await my punishment.

✦ ✦ ✦

With an involuntary scream, I regained consciousness again, reeling from a major head injury. I rolled off my back and down onto all fours, gasping for breath through thick layers of a scarf. I yanked it away from my mouth. But my first full breath brought the fiery pain that only very cold air can produce, so I arranged the woolen scarf back over my nose and mouth. Until a moment ago, I had been soaked in warm Cambodian rainwater and my own blood, from a gunshot to the chest. So it was out with the bloody lung and the steamy monsoon, in with the bad brain and the extreme cold. And I hated cold!

    I slowly lowered my thickly-wrapped forehead onto grimy snow, to endure the familiar anguish and the unfamiliar bashed head. No, no, no, not again, my dazed mind shouted; but that throbbing, silent scream was subsiding rapidly. My fate had long been obvious. So as the pain of my death in Cambodia subsided, my fear of this new situation faded, even before I knew what it would be.

    The air and ground were deeply cold. I was deeply cold, too; but it was wearing off. I was warming slightly, like a new fire started in a long-cold woodstove. With my eyes still closed and my forehead still on the icy ground, I took inventory of my other physical sensations. The left side of my head had definitely been injured, but that was at the end of someone else's life. The pain and fog were clearing rapidly. I tried opening and closing my jaw and discovered the left joint of my jaw was still healing. Not dislocated, but painful from a fractured skull through the upper jawbone that was knitting back together quickly.

    My toes and fingers burned with cold, which meant they weren't frostbitten. Slowly, I moved my left hand to the side of my head and felt the layer of fluid under the scalp and around my left ear. It was the last remnant of this poor schmuck's fatal head wound, apparently. But overall, I felt surprisingly fit. I checked myself again. My jaw worked normally and my head wound now was healed.

I pushed myself up onto my knees, and looked through the narrow scarf opening. It was barely light, as though the sun was low in the sky, which was heavy with thick clouds. There were two dead soldiers in the hole with me, lightly covered with frost. We were all in the same uniform: white parkas and pants, thick gloves and scarves, and thick leather boots with oddly upturned toes. Fascinated by the strange boots, I examined the closest boot on one of my dead comrades. The instep of the boot had a thick layer of leather sewn onto it, and both that upper layer and the entire toe of the boot was curved upward sharply, as if to grasp something. I was puzzled by that, immensely so.

Otherwise, we were in an icy hole typical of a far-north machine-gun nest. There were miniature craters in the hole and on one side wall from the impact of bullets. The nest had apparently been built hurriedly from soil and packed snow, all wetted at some point, and now frozen solid as concrete. There was a pine forest outside the hole, with a snow-covered road nearby. Obviously, this nest was intended to cover the road.

I searched through the clothing of the two bodies. I was hungry, but I wasn't yet sure what I was looking for, other than food. I couldn't avoid wondering when

I'd last eaten in Cambodia, but of course that counted for nothing here.

Both bodies had bullet holes through their torsos. I looked over my uniform and I had no such holes. "So I just got it in the head. Right, boys?" I asked my two former comrades. "And you strong, silent types won't even tell me where I am!"

The bodies were frozen stiff, as though they'd been there many days. I supposed I had been also, but I suppressed the thought. Under the white parkas, both men had little in their pockets, but I did find a paper-wrapped crust of bread in one man's gray tunic, and an aluminum water bottle with a small amount of ice in it. The other man's civilian-looking undercoat contained two small, unmarked cans, apparently bulging from frozen contents. I opened my scarf enough to hold the piece of bread in my mouth, then closed the scarf around it. I unscrewed the cap of the water bottle, stuffed the bottle full of snow, replaced the cap, and tucked it into one of the larger pockets of my gray tunic. In a few hours, maybe I'd have a small quantity of water. Then I put the cans into one of my other tunic pockets, noticing it was very similar to the other man's uniform tunic. Only then I realized I hadn't searched my pockets yet. I found only another piece of bread and a small folding knife which didn't appear to be a good tool for opening cans.

I sat in the bottom of the hole with my back against the icy side and ate the piece of bread that I'd been holding in my mouth. It was frozen hard, and it must have been dense black bread even before becoming frozen, so eating it wasn't easy. After I tore loose each small chunk, I put a little snow in my mouth, then waited for the bread to become moistened. We had been told to never eat unmelted snow that way, during some life in the now-distant past. But in some small number of minutes, hours, or days, I'd probably experience much worse. So I had no immediate concern about hypothermia.

As I ate, I observed that the machine-gun nest seemed to be especially bare. No machine gun, no rifles, no ammunition, and no packs. Just us three bodies, frozen blood puddles, lots of fired cartridge cases, and a little dirty snow. So either the nest had been hurriedly picked clean, or the machine-gun crew had hidden their equipment and supplies. Or maybe friendly forces had been there, recovered weapons and equipment, but they couldn't recover the bodies. If they couldn't recover the bodies, then maybe they were traveling light, and had only hidden the weapons from the enemy. They couldn't have buried anything in the ground; there was no way to dig. But the drifted snow behind the nest could hide almost anything.

After I finished the bread, I checked the road and forest to be sure I was alone, and I felt around in the drifted snow around the nest. There wasn't much on the road side, where I re-packed and smoothed the snow after I'd searched it. But behind the nest, my arms sank into deeper snow. I scooped the snow out of a hole with my heavily gloved hands, and found what I was looking for. I placed each item into the front of the nest as I found it. Soon it became apparent the hole was a trench which led from the back of the nest into the forest. It was small and shallow, maybe two feet deep and two feet wide. After the first six feet, the trench contained only drifted-in snow. So maybe the trench had been planned as an escape route and dug before the ground had become frozen.

Back in the nest, I wrestled each of the bodies over the short back wall and into the trench, as much as they would fit into it. Then I smoothed the snow over them, to disguise their presence. Next, I inventoried the items I'd found.

There were three pairs of skis and ski poles, but they were unbelievably crude. The skis were made only of formed wood and leather straps. I arranged the skis and poles behind the nest in sets, ready for quick use in case I learned how to use them. On a hunch, I pulled one of the skis back into the nest, rolled onto my back, and checked it for fit onto one of my boots. I could hook the upturned toe of my boot under the shorter, double-thickness leather strap, and the other strap seemed to be made to fit around my ankle. Together, the straps would allow my foot to flex over the ski to permit cross-country skiing. With that little mystery solved, I placed the ski back outside the nest.

Next, I considered the weapons I'd found. There were two bolt-action rifles and one crude, heavy automatic. I picked up one of the bolt-action rifles and wiped away more of the snow stuck to it. The rifle was amazingly long and primitive. It looked like something from the nineteenth century, but I couldn't identify its type. I tried to work the action, but the bolt had been wet, probably after having been dropped into snow soon after it had last been fired. Now the entire receiver was frozen together, as solidly as if it had been welded. It couldn't function until I found a way to warm it. The other bolt-action rifle was in the same condition, so I placed them outside the nest, beside the skis.

Having a long-developed admiration of firepower, I was quick to examine the large automatic rifle. It looked like a distant relative of the Browning automatic rifle, with a similar 20-round box magazine. I released the obvious catch behind the magazine and the magazine dropped from the rifle. I picked it up and checked it. It was empty so I placed it on the edge of the nest. I worked the bolt a few times, and soon it moved easily.

But the muzzle was packed with snow. Remembering the bolt-action rifles had cleaning rods under their barrels, I retrieved one and extracted its cleaning rod. In a few minutes, the barrel of the automatic rifle was cleared. I put the cleaning rod back into the bolt-action rifle. Then, on an impulse, I pushed it into the trench muzzle-downward, near the two frozen bodies. Its plain wooden stock wouldn't be conspicuous from the road, with the forest in the background. But the rifle might serve as a marker for the two dead Soldiers.

    I returned to the automatic rifle. Because I had hands-on experience with so many types of weapons, I knew how to proceed. I fiddled with the safety switch until I understood how it worked, based on which position allowed the familiar "click" when I pulled the trigger. Then I identified the full-auto position of the fire selector lever, by repeating the test while holding the trigger back as I racked the bolt. I then carefully balanced it on the side of the nest, so it wouldn't fall into the snow.

    There were now three packs remaining, which seemed to be primitive civilian backpacks of different designs. One had six full twenty-round magazines for the automatic rifle and a pair of wool socks. Another had ten five-round clips, apparently containing the same type of cartridge, and more wool socks. But there didn't seem to be any way to strip the clips into the magazines, as is done with US M16s and M4s. Finally, I decided the clips must go directly into the old bolt-action rifles. The third backpack had five empty automatic rifle magazines, more 5-round clips, and two German-style potato-masher grenades with wooden handles. A third grenade had a similar handle, but it had a huge, boxy, sheet-metal head. The green paint on the sheet metal was fresh, so the huge grenade hadn't been carried long. It was heavy and obviously very deadly. Maybe an anti-tank grenade? It must have weighed ten pounds!

    I decided to learn how to set it off. So I carefully unscrewed the cap from the end of the handle and even more carefully pulled the cap off. When I did, a white ceramic bead dropped about an inch from the end of the handle, retained by a lanyard. My hair stood on end for a second, but then I realized the bead would need to be pulled to activate the fuse. I turned the huge grenade upside-down and balanced the bead in the hollow handle. Then I screwed the cap back on, very gingerly, and placed all three grenades on the edge of the nest.

    Next, I forced one of the cartridges out of a five-round clip and compared it with one from a twenty-round magazine. Their headstamps were different, but there was no doubt they were the same cartridge type and interchangeable. So I removed enough cartridges from the five-round clips to fill the empty twenty-round magazines. The cartridges were rimmed, so they had to be placed so that the rim of an upper cartridge was always to the front of the one below. Also, stuffing cartridges into the primitive magazines was ridiculously difficult, because the magazine springs were far too strong, especially for loading with cold fingers. But I finally finished and was glad to be rid of that task.

That flurry of activity—and frustration—warmed all of me, except my feet, my abused fingers, and where the aluminum water bottle was near my belly. So I decided to check around the area. I placed a full magazine into the automatic rifle and racked its bolt to chamber a round. I put the other ten full magazines into a backpack, then swung it onto my back. I hopped up and down slightly for a noise check and the magazines in the backpack made more noise than I would have thought possible. So I'd have to walk carefully or repack the backpack with some kind of insulating material between the magazines to move silently. Or more likely, gently dump the backpack long before any encounter with the enemy—whoever that might turn out to be.

I picked up the loaded automatic rifle and retrieved one of the ski poles to use as a walking stick. I checked all around again, looking and listening, and then carefully walked toward the road. Most of the snow was hard and icy beyond the tree line and I left no footprints on it.

Closer to the road, the snow became powdery again, and it squeaked metallically with each step. There was a uniform drift of snow on the closer edge of the road, about four feet wide, slightly sunken. I was concerned there might be a ditch under the snow, and I would leave deep footprints. So I turned the ski pole over, and held it by its spoked, round foot. I then probed the snow by pushing the handle end into it, leaving a relatively inconspicuous hole. The snow was deep! So probed other places, and soon found there was a foxhole beside the road, filled with drifted snow, and at least three feet deep. Amazing! Or was it some kind of tank trap? Wanting to mark it, at least temporarily, I used the pointed tip of the ski pole to make some slight boundary lines. I thought the lines wouldn't be noticed by anyone else.

I then crossed the drift, away from the foxhole, and then used the ski pole to smooth the powder. That done, I checked the road surface carefully. There were all kinds of tracks in the granular snow there: tracked vehicles, wheeled vehicles, horses with shoes on their hooves, and men on foot. Was this the 1930s or 1940s? There were varying amounts of fresh snow in the many types of tracks, so the road was used regularly. And there was no doubt this was a busy road, at least intermittently. I looked both ways on the road, more suspicious now than ever. Had the sky brightened, or was there just more of the low light out in the open?

Looking among the treetops, the deep silence of the place became fully apparent. There was not the slightest breath of wind and the trees seemed to be impenetrable barriers of sound. More than that, they seemed to be actively absorbing the slightest noise I made. I imagined how a bird flying over could be clearly heard within this vacuum of sound, but there were no birds. Finally, it occurred to me that the place had the extreme silence of a no-man's land, between two dangerous opponents, cautiously and temporarily at rest. Like the Ardennes had been before that brutal German counterattack. I shuddered with the recollection of a previous death there, under a Panzer IV.

The road was curved slightly in both directions, so visibility along the road was limited. There was no indication of the sun's direction in the gloomy sky, so I wasn't sure which way was north. I wasn't even sure which hemisphere I was in, but the northern hemisphere seemed to be a safe bet. Maybe the sun would be visible later, I hoped.

I looked toward the machine-gun nest; it was barely visible. The grenades were visible on the front rim of the nest, so I'd certainly have to move them. But the nest itself had been well placed behind the first few trees of the forest, an excellent distance from the road. It blended well into the background, which was irregular due to various contours of snow. I assumed the lumps were fallen trees and stumps, but it was impossible to know without digging around in the forest.

The bad news was that some of the trees on one side of the nest had damage from bullets, high on their trunks, in bright yellow. The damaged trees might draw attention to the area around the nest, I first thought. But as I checked the entire area more carefully, I saw there were chips knocked out of other trees. So there had been a firefight; more than just a few trees had been damaged, and the nest's location wasn't necessarily made obvious after all.

I checked my footprints; they were very conspicuous. The ice and snow on the road had been churned into a sand-textured, crunching grit since the last thaw. I backed off the road, using the ski pole to camouflage my tracks, trying to match the other patterns of tracks. The result didn't look good, but my tracks were less noticeable.

I then moved back to the machine-gun nest, smoothing the snow along the way, and grounded the noisy backpack. I thought about those cans of food while checking the water bottle. The ice and snow in it were still unmelted. I placed it back into my tunic pocket. Looking around again, I considered relocating. It seemed impractical to stay in the nest, but traveling on the road seemed too dangerous to contemplate. Skiing through the forest was a possibility, but where would I go if I didn't find a trail? More to the point: should I choose a possible sudden death by the road or a longer freezing struggle in the forest? That was an easy call.

While I was thinking about improving the nest, I heard engine noise. I stopped all motion and breathing and listened. The engine sound faded away twice, then came back stronger. It sounded like a truck being driven in low gear.

The familiar dread before battle flowed through me. The possible alternatives to fighting flashed through my mind. I hated being wounded in the cold. So I briefly entertained the idea of finishing this one quickly and moving to the next situation. But I quickly rejected any such notion. I'd never been the type for suicide. And surrendering wasn't EVER an option after what the Sioux had done to me. Even trying to hide in the frigid forest seemed to be a bad idea. So time for the fight!

I pulled the full magazines from the backpack, flattened it on the floor of the nest, and arranged the magazines on top of it. After placing the two regular grenades beside the magazines I set the giant grenade beside the backpack, handle pointing upward.

The source of the engine noise was getting closer, but there was nothing visible on the road. I decided I should do more to prepare. Removing the caps from the handles of all the grenades, I was pleased to see they all had the same kind of ceramic bead hanging from the same type of lanyard. Next, I removed the water bottle from my tunic and tossed it to the back of the nest. I checked my boots and uniform; everything seemed secure. Pulling the white parka hood over my face as low as it would go, I grabbed the automatic rifle and settled down into the nest, facing the road.

The machine was coming closer, but the vehicle still wasn't visible. It gradually became clear that it was approaching from my left and that it was something really noisy. I scooted slightly left, flipped the safety catch to the "Fire" position, and tugged my parka hood lower again. I needed to have as much white over my face as possible because the scarf was a dull gray.

I waited much longer than I had expected and the cold soaked into my front. Eventually, the machine came into view. It was a tank, not a truck! Not good! But maybe a tank would be easier to identify than a truck, and then I might have some clue where and when I was. But as the tank slowly came closer, I had no idea what type it was. There was a heavy stub on the far side of the turret, and a machine gun pointing out of the opposite side. That made no sense! There didn't seem to be a barrel for the tank's main gun at all. And the tank was dark green! Who operates a dark green tank in snow country? Then, as it came closer, I saw that the stubby side also had a machine gun. Then I knew the crew must have their machine guns facing to both sides of the road to guard against ambushes. Not good, again!

As the tank came closer still, I saw there was a small group of infantry following the tank. The leader seemed to be trying to get his troops to catch up, but the tank was going too fast for them. Disregarding their infantry support meant the tank crew was scared and stupid. The infantry, only seven of them, were in khaki pants with tall brown boots, brown jackets, and green helmets. What idiots! Only the Soviets would shamelessly disregard their troops to that degree. That had to be it! I was an honorary Finn, in the Winter War! So was this late 1939 or early 1940?

No, I shouldn't try to remember the details, I answered myself. I had to focus on that situation. But why wasn't the infantry riding on the tank?

As the tank came closer, I could see the stubby side of the turret was facing more toward the opposite side of the road than the side having only the machine gun. That seemed in my favor, and the obvious plan came to mind; a plan that wasn't half bad against that primitive-looking tank!

I saw the right front fender had been torn from the tank, above the right track. The green paint had been scorched black in that same area. That made me wonder if the tank had been repaired, and it was traveling to rejoin its unit. In any case, their journey certainly wasn't part of an attack. Advantage back to me!

Very, very slowly, I shifted the automatic rifle to a good point to fire on the infantry. I knew any sudden motion might attract someone's attention. As for the tank, with its turret in a front-left, back-right position, I thought I might be in one of their blind spots.

I was quivering, but no longer from cold. I made an effort to settle my nerves and focus. Focus! The leader of the infantry was slightly ahead of the others and his followers didn't seem to be with the program. In fact, their misery and dread was plain to see and they were clumped far too close together. Fools! But don't worry, Comrades, I thought, your suffering will soon be over. I was then into position, with the leader about to walk into my line of fire.

Then, he was in my sights, just as the tank was approaching the point on the road closest to the nest. I pulled the heavy trigger briefly, and the automatic rifle spat out a short burst with a perfect cadence. The leader was down, but as I shifted left to the followers, I saw they were down too. They were sucking snow, too panicked to move off the road! So I fired two more bursts into their concentrated clump, and I could see the bullets throwing up snow around them and past them. Good hits!

I quickly dumped the magazine, not caring how many rounds I'd fired, loaded a full one, and racked the bolt. I really dreaded what came next. Screaming myself to death, yet again, was now a very real possibility.

I grabbed the huge grenade and, still carrying the automatic rifle, I jumped out of the nest and ran toward the tank. The race was on!

The tank had stopped directly to the front of the nest and I could see the stubby part of the turret turning toward me. Only then, I could see the stub was actually its main gun, with a short little barrel! My legs pumped with a fresh shot of adrenaline. The machine gun beside the stubby main gun began to fire as I fell and landed hard in deep snow. I had forgotten the foxhole beside the road and I'd fallen into it! There was a huge explosion, then another one. Apparently the stubby, low-velocity main gun had been fired at the nest, probably blowing it to atoms. I scrambled out of the snow and out of the hole. I was still clutching the huge grenade, but I'd somehow dropped the automatic rifle.

The machine gun was firing over my head as I quickly crawled to the tank, staying low. In a couple of seconds I was beside the tank's right track. I yanked the ceramic bead of the huge grenade. The bead, the lanyard, and a steel pin all came out of the hollow handle. Like an idiot, I looked at them, wondering if that was normal or if I'd broken the damned thing. Then I came to my senses and stood just enough to toss the grenade onto the back deck of the tank, behind the turret. I didn't wait around to see if it remained in place. I dropped to the ground, rolled back into the foxhole, and tried to swim down into the snow.

The explosion was enormous, worse than when the tank's main gun fired. It was absolutely stunning—But I didn't have time for that. With my ears ringing loudly, I flailed around in the snow, blindly trying to find the automatic rifle.

I finally found it. I got a good grip on it, raised it to my shoulder, and prepared to fire. But I still couldn't see! I swiped the scarf off my head hurriedly; staying warm didn't matter in that moment. It seemed I had taken far too long, but as I faced the tank, the right turret crewmember was emerging from it only then. My mind hesitated because the barrel might be full of snow again, but my trigger finger did not. I fired a burst into him. He screamed and quickly slumped onto the side of his hatch opening. The flat deck of the tank, behind the turret, was already burning fiercely. The tank must have been powered by gasoline to burn so readily.

Knowing I was in the wrong place, I scrambled from the foxhole again and made a running crawl to the front of the tank. I stopped on one knee, so close to the front of the tank that I hoped the driver couldn't see me. The left turret hatch flipped open and the driver's hatch opened a split second later. The driver was pushing his hatch open with his feet, so I shifted to the left turret.

Comrade Left Turret had been expecting me to still be in the foxhole, so he had emerged with a submachine gun pointed in that direction. I was able to shoot him before he could turn to me. The driver's hatch was then locked open, so I fired into its inner surface, hoping for ricochet hits, or at least to keep the driver's head down.

But how many more were in the tank?

I shifted right to what had been the far side of the tank, raised the automatic rifle, and checked on the infantry. They were all still, except one who had only been wounded; he was crawling off the road without his rifle. So I turned back to the turret. There was a machine gun also on the back side, opposite the stubby main gun. What was this thing?! No wonder there were no riders. This thing had machine guns on both the front and rear of the turret!

Avoiding the back-side machine gun and the now-roaring flames on the rear deck, I climbed onto the forward end of the left track, then stepped onto the left fender. With a better angle into the driver's and left turret hatches, I quickly fired a burst into each. Comrade Right Turret hadn't moved. There was no more movement or noise, except for the growing fire. And there were no more hatches.

I turned the automatic rifle back to the infantry to check them again. One of their weapons moved, and I tried to fire. But nothing happened. I was out of ammo!

There was a shout to my left and I swung the automatic rifle to the left instinctively, even though it was empty. The figure there was in a white camouflage uniform like mine, on skis, and he was holding his rifle over his head.

More Finns excitedly skied from the forest, all shouting gibberish I didn't understand. Had I done something wrong?

But then I could see there were smiles behind the scarves, and I realized they were mad with joy. I threw my arms up, shouting as they were, intending to hold the automatic rifle over my head. But my snow-crusted gloves lost their grip on it and the rifle flew back over my head. Not caring, I shouted even louder!

I turned right to see some of the Finns running around the tank; they were firing similar automatic rifles into the remnants of the Soviet infantry. I shouted another "Hoo-Rah!" as three of the Finns pulled me from the tank and carried me up the road on their shoulders. Then they dropped me onto my feet, and were WAY too damn kissy. But my elation was complete and I knew I loved war!

THAT was my sin, permanent and unforgivable! I loved war! I had first said that foolishly, in some fast-food joint in Iraq, or in a coffee shop on some US airbase in Afghanistan. Damnable, unpardonable, forever. But it was true!

I took the bottle that was offered and took a huge gulp of the clear liquid inside it. I choked disgusting, ice-cold, captured Soviet vodka onto my hairy chin. I gasped for air, then shouted with joy again. I knew I'd die painfully and pathetically again very soon; then I'd be on to the next horrible battle, in some horrible place, in some horrible time. But I didn't care! That perfect moment was complete, except for one nagging question:

Was this Heaven, or Hell?

PLANET OF IDIOTS

The third rail of contemporary science fiction writing is apparently making one's aliens too human-like. I can't decide whether that's an unintended result of decades of "Forehead Theater," where the aliens are instantly recognizable as DIFFERENT only due to the cheap make-up on their faces, or some reflexive (and totally understandable) rejection of the "Forehead Theater" concept.

Regardless which is the case, logic and reason must prevail. For example, are one's aliens legit only if a story is thirty pages of apparently random symbols? Does a story make sense only if the aliens *exhibit a long series of incomprehensible behaviors, toward no discernable end? Of course not.*

Furthermore, if my aliens (very soon to be our aliens, I promise) are members of a society driven by technology and the usual (i.e. unavoidable) level of bureaucracy, why wouldn't we share some characteristics with them? How could we not? Are technology and bureaucracy not the great, crushing wheels which grind us all down to uniformity?

Finally, wouldn't a reader need to develop some sympathy, share some kind of well-founded dread, or at least develop some level of understanding with the aliens to become invested into the story? Of course! That was the original essence of science fiction, all those decades ago. Naturally, that necessity still exists.

Still, my purpose—and my obligation—here is to find some way to push at the edges of what's expected or allowed. Otherwise, dear readers would not be amused, and we can't have that!

So, beyond the inevitable similarities of the aliens involved, what if the immediate setting for Earth's conquest isn't aboard ray-gun shooting rocket ships, on the beach where the scary monster walks ashore, or any of the other well-worn locations? If we share any level of technical bureaucracy with aliens, why wouldn't it be the lowly and humble conference room?

The editor of the *Fredan Mountain Record* stared in disgust at his youngest reporter, yapping on across the table, his excitement gradually building toward pee-puddle intensity. The young pup still hadn't grown his facial whiskers, he still had no grey in his coat, and—as usual—his latest story made no sense at all. The kid was even too young to have been in the war, thought the editor with sharp disdain. And to make the situation worse, his deputy editor, Danne, was leaning back on the couch beside him, making odd noises. Anyone who erroneously believed Danne might be able to restrain himself might also be thinking he was getting sick, or something.

"Wait," said the editor, interrupting enthusiastic gibberish coming from his cub reporter. "Tell me again how he was talking to the aliens. The equipment, he was using, I mean."

"Like I said before, it was a surplus radio from an old mail service airplane. And he said the aliens' signal was strongest on 120 kilocycles. The—"

Danne made some kind of choking noise.

"Sorry, tell me again about the antenna he was using with that."

"He called it a dipole. But the aliens—"

"What's a dipole?"

"It was two lengths of aluminum wire going in opposite directions from his cabin. The ends were stretched to the two adjacent ridgelines. It would take a full day to walk from one end of the antenna to the other, up and down the mountains. But when the aliens called back—"

Danne whined like he was in pain.

"Danne, give it a rest," groaned the editor. "My head hurts so much, it feels like my whiskers are about to fall out. Let me try to understand the kid."

"But you have to understand!" demanded the young reporter. "He told me about prime numbers, and the aliens continued a series of them! He sent two beeps, then three, five, and seven. Then the aliens sent back eleven beeps!"

"How long did it take for the answer to come back?"

"A few minutes."

Danne blurted out the beginning of a howl like he had just treed a rock bear, then locked his muzzle closed with both hands.

"Look, kid. Leave the copy of your notes and let us decide how to run this. Shut up, Danne." Danne's head had already popped up in surprise.

"Write up a draft of your story like the guy's maybe a little crazy and you weren't sure what to believe."

"But—"

"Trust me, kid. Now get to work. I want the first draft of your story within the hour. Listen to me: 300 words maximum. We have a deadline. If you want your story in this morning's paper, which I know very well you do, you have to get me the story right away. Now get out of here, and get to work!"

The kid gathered up his papers, dropped the photo-chemical copies of his notes, and walked out of the editor's office. His bushy tail was between his legs, as it usually was after a meeting with his editor, despite his story of a lifetime.

"Close the door, please!" called the editor. The reporter did, gently, as to not show offense.

Danne was suddenly talkative. "You're not going to run that excrement, are you?"

"What else do I have?" The editor raised up a sheaf of the previous evening's teletypewriter print-outs, and dropped them back onto his desk like they were a useless pile of leaves. "It's past midnight, and there's nothing of interest in this stuff. And what other local stories do we have? You want me to get excited about the obituaries?"

"But you understand how long it takes for radio waves to travel into space, and a reply to come back. And an old mail-plane radio? Please!"

"Look, we'll run it like the old guy is some kind of crank. He's most likely talking with some other mountaintop hermit, who has another mail-plane radio, two or three mountains over."

"They'll laugh at us!"

"No, they won't, if he comes off as just an oddball. What do I care if someone laughs? Just make sure we don't get sued by those two mountain-top radio operators! Now go help the pup with his story!"

It would later be discovered there was only the one radio operator, and he was indeed communicating with aliens—of a kind. And they were not even two mountains away. But aliens from a distant planet had also heard the telegraphy transmissions, among millions of other Fredan radio emissions, and time was quickly running out. The Fredans had less than four years left to live.

The "Old One" listened to the endless background noise of the galaxy and cursed his unending isolation. Time passed. The white noise, the amalgamation of countless unknown electro-magnetic sources, continued as always. The faint hiss reminded him of the background noise deep within his home mountain range. Except this noise was uninterrupted by the thoughts of others like him, deep in the layers of the mountains. More than ever, he missed their ultra-low radio-frequency fellowship.

More time passed, longer than the lifetime of a Goll. His hatred of the Golls grew more intense and he wished every one of them condemned to eternal suffering. Then he thought, self-mockingly: no, the place of eternal suffering is here in this ship, and it's much better they're not here! He took a long moment's satisfaction in being rid of the little vermin for all of time.

He was mounted into the nose of the Goll-designed ship, still surrounded by remnants of the crystalline rock in which he had originally been formed. He and that rock around him had been permanently encased in an alumino-silicate fiber composite shell, gradually applied as he had been excavated from his mountain. And all that had been bonded into a custom cradle of gigantic aluminum beams, mounting him rigidly into the ship's conical nose structure. Electromagnetic probes had been carefully installed into the composite shell at the points calculated to be most efficient for interface purposes. The probes, of course, were his two-way links to the ship's interface array.

He recalled how the Golls had recruited him and his fellows for this mission. Their urgent pleas, through the ground-penetrating interface invented by the native Fredans, indicated their desperation. Only the "Old Ones" could perform this reconnaissance mission, the Golls said, due to their indefinite lifespans. The "Old Ones" negotiated long and hard, being distrustful, mostly because his home planet's Fredans suddenly became extinct soon after the arrival of the Golls.

Finally, enough "Old Ones" agreed to take part in the mission. The Golls had never realized the new pilot recruits were those most shallow in their mountains, and motivated to escape the deadly, rapidly-approaching erosion. Under the terms of the agreement, the "Old Ones" remaining in place would be wealthy forever, in secure Galactic Credits, and their home mountains protected and guarded.

Soon the pilot recruits were mined from their mountains and transported to the Goll home world. Even more quickly—for them, it seemed—they were installed into their ships, had their interface probes attached, and their individual interface programs with their ships' solid-state interface arrays were developed using adaptive software. The interface included his virtual mission display panel, existing only as a virtual object within his mind. It seemed extremely intrusive at first. But it rapidly became familiar, then welcome, during the mission training he received next. The first steps were interoperability and calibration checks with the passive radio direction-finder antenna array, which was had been built into the ship's nose and its outer skin. Transmitter and engine control systems checks followed. In what seemed to be just an instant, the preparations were completed. The "Old One" relished his new senses through and beyond the ship.

As each became ready, their ships were launched. Each departed into one of the 100 assigned spherical sectors from the Goll world, on the mission until the end of time.

Now, after so much time, he hated his monotonous mission. In its cruise profile, the ship's navigation and maintenance functions were simple. So he spent most of his time just listening to the soft incoherence of the galaxy. The boredom and isolation became worse moment by moment, each the passing of yet more generations of the Golls. Worse still, he knew the space beyond the edge of this galaxy would be even more quiet and empty, until the nearest edge of the next galaxy approached.

Still more time passed.

He heard an intermittent buzzing noise, but it faded away. It was so faint he wasn't sure it had been real, but he thought its strangeness made it unlikely to be a product of his long-tortured imagination. There was no signal data displayed, so maybe it was. Later, he heard a similar signal. It was more clearly above the galactic background noise than the first one. It was bursts of static, obviously switched on and off in some coded format. The discovery of an artificial signal, after so much time, was disturbing in a way he hadn't expected. Was this something ominous, or had he only adapted to his completely monotonous existence? And why was there still no signal data?

Suddenly, his virtual monitor panel automatically zoomed to an obscure point in space, which was then highlighted in a color he hadn't seen since his training. Then, he remembered. Signal data wouldn't be displayed until an algorithm had differentiated the signal from natural emissions, and the interface had determined a bearing to the source. He selected the highlighted source, then the two-dimensional bearing data was displayed.

At first, the bearing numbers appeared to be random digits without meaning. Having been obtained with so much time, effort, and expense, the sets of numbers seemed strangely ordinary. The "Old One" dismissed that reaction, selected the bearing numbers, and applied them to the navigation display. The bearing was only slightly off his base course line. Good, he thought, the most basic validity check was satisfied. A source to the ship's front would probably be relevant to the mission. The display also showed the signal to be independent of the slight emissions of the ship's electrical systems and ion drives.

He opened the signal detection checklist on his monitor and re-read the protocol he'd studied so many times before. From that, he opened the signal report form and began entering data. The form would serve as the source for a coded packet to be transmitted to the Golls' home world, again using a carefully controlled directional beam, sent at minimum power. The packet would be retransmitted at slightly higher power, incrementally increasing in strength until an acknowledgment code was received. The form required data for source triangulation, which he didn't yet have, so more time passed.

While waiting, he considered the special transmitter on board. All aspects of its design, construction, and performance were closely guarded secrets. During his training, the Golls refused to hear any questions about it. Yet, he reasoned, it must have a capability beyond light speed. The signals he detected were already traveling toward the Goll home world at light speed and they were probably strong enough to eventually get there. So if the ship's transmissions weren't faster than light, the recon ships wouldn't have been necessary.

In time, the one signal became many. He began to hear various tones of continuous-wave telegraphy. At first they were chirpy and distorted, but eventually became cleaner and faster beeps. Amplitude-modulated signals containing some unintelligible gibberish could also be tracked. The ship's path served as the baseline for triangulating the source of the signals, with a long series of bearings necessary. All that data went into page after page of the report form, until the triangulation requirements were satisfied. The "Old One" was impressed by the quality of the data. The data collection process was straightforward and the correlation of the triangulation data was excellent.

The "Old One" wasn't concerned with decoding the telegraphy or understanding the primitive gibberish. That was the responsibility of the Golls and he hoped the problem would perplex and torment them. He wondered, briefly, about the fate of the beings sending the signals. But they weren't his responsibility either, and beings stupid enough to give away their position deserved whatever they got. He assumed their fate would be the same as the long-dead Fredans, without dwelling on it.

He initiated transmission of the report, checked that the event had been captured in the automated ship's log, and set an automatic alert for when the acknowledgement from the Golls was received. He mapped an adjusted course to keep the ship an undetectable distance from the source and adjusted the ion drive.

Then, with the work complete for his first signal source, he began his search for the next. He felt much better about his mission, at least for the following eon or two.

Devron, like most Golls, had more than one job.

He spent most of his time as a Quality Control Manager in a company which manufactured ceramic parts for spacecraft. He liked the mathematical rigor and precision of component testing, mostly performing ultrasonic resonance tests for flaws inside ceramic materials. Designing tests for new parts was interesting to him. Parts with new shapes needed careful evaluation for full saturation of ultrasonic energy across a wide spectrum in order to detect defects of various types and sizes. He liked maintaining strict control over his inspectors while constantly monitoring their efficiency. He liked conning Galactic Credits from them whenever silly rumors or their occasional gullibility made them vulnerable in the office betting pools. But most of all, he liked his salary and his profit sharing.

His other job as a ship manager in the Space Service Reserve carried more responsibility, but had a minimal probability of profit. Sometimes he wondered why he bothered. Most of his family said he was wasting his time in the Service because so many Golls had served their entire working lives based on the promise of fantastic profits, but had received nothing but a modest part-time salary. Still, monitoring his assigned electromagnetic reconnaissance ship didn't take much time; the pay for the few hours he worked was good, and he took pride in his title. He hoped his work could be passed to his descendants. His ship had been monitored by four generations of a different Goll family before it had been assigned to him.

Every standard month, he prepared a report detailing his ship's projected position and sent it to his commanding manager, Lofann. Because his ship had not yet produced a radio report, except for the communications checks at the beginning of the mission, no other data was available. So each report was only a single chart showing the ship's estimated progress within its spherical sector, together with known galactic features.

Lofann examined each chart carefully. That Devron could understand. What he couldn't understand was Lofann's obsession with every imagined hazard or anomaly, even though the ship's estimated position was little more than guesswork.

So it came as no surprise when his monitor at the factory showed an incoming call from Lofann. More useless discussion about percentages of trajectory deviation caused by passing gravitational sources, or some other nonsense, he thought. He selected the call.

"Devron," he reported.

"Greetings, Devron. It's Lofann," came the reply. "I'll be direct. Your ship has transmitted a signal source report. You are ordered to active duty for one month to process a report to Space Command Central, and then serve as my liaison while they decide what to do about it. Is this information about your civilian job still correct?"

The image of Lofann was replaced with his completed Standard Form 368, "Civilian Employment Status for Processing Involuntary Mobilization," which Devron had hoped he'd never have to see again. It was part of a set of documents he was required to keep ready for the unexpected.

"Everything is still current," he replied. "When do I need to report?"

"Stand by."

Devron waited, with both his dread and excitement building. Lofann's head—together with his excessively serrated, oddly graying brow antennae—was suddenly on the monitor again.

"I just submitted your packet for Space Service leave to your employer and copied you. Talk to your manager there if you have questions on their end. Report tomorrow morning at the sixth hour in my office at the Joint Reserve Center. I want to send up your initial report by the end of the first day, so be ready to work. Bring your overnight bag, too. Expect Central to have follow-up questions about your report. I want you to stay here in the JRC until they're happy with it, even if that takes days. After that, you can report back in every day at the sixth hour until they're done with us completely. If it turns out to take longer than a month, I'll have your orders extended. Questions?"

"Too many for right now."

"Good. I'll see you at six." The call dropped.

Just great, Devron thought. His excitement had ebbed. His dread had not.

As happened so many times in the service, the plan changed. By the third day, Devron was in the Space Service Central complex, deep under the tallest mountain range in the Goll's home world.

After being cleared into the complex, he walked the entrance hall, looking for cross-corridor 47. The main hall was almost empty, which was surprising. The markings in the raw white granite indicated the hall was originally a large round tunnel, with material later removed to flatten the floor. The white granite brightened the hall, which had only scattered overhead lights. Devron noticed the cable trays on the walls were full with glass fiber cables, indicating a massive communications capability into the rest of the planet's tunnel systems.

After finding corridor 47, a tunnel to the right, he found the correct conference room and entered. It was empty, but there was a carafe of hot water and cups on the counter at the end of the room. There was also a package of nutrition biscuits. But without being in his feeding cycle, the very thought of the biscuits made his guts heave. He poured a cup of hot water, chose a place at the side of the long table opposite the door, and settled into a comfortable squat on the floor.

In a short time, three others entered the room. Devron assumed the formal greeting pose of the Service, standing erect with all his arms at his side.

"Be seated," said the oldest who entered, who seemed accustomed to having Golls standing for his entrances. Devron recognized him as Croom, a former member of the Space Service Board of Directors. Croom walked to the counter and poured himself a hot drink.

The others squatted across the table from Devron, who resumed his place.

"Greetings, Devron. I see you've helped yourself. Anyone else want a hot drink?"

They didn't.

"Then may I assume no one is within their feeding cycle?" Croom asked.

The answer was a slightly uneasy silence.

"Good!"

Croom squatted at the head of the table nearest the counter, settling slowly on his lower abdominal segments, as older Golls usually did. He took a sip from his drink and took a moment to savor it, which seemed to demonstrate an unhurried, methodical nature in his actions. He put the cup down and turned to Devron.

"I am Croom. I've been named project manager for an off-planet expedition which might have promise. You might remember I was on the Board until two years ago, and it seems I didn't mess that up too badly. That made me eligible to lead an off-planet project of interest and here it is."

"Greetings", replied Devron.

Croom sipped from his cup again, then continued: "With me are Whele, manager of the Space Service, and Untat, my deputy manager for this project."

"Greetings," they both said.

"Devron, we've all read your report. It's well-written and your data is in order. We've read your personnel file too. Here's the situation: a ship manager in the Reserve has specific duties when a report comes in. But for now, you're mobilized indefinitely and there's another job to do. We need you to serve as the Space Service project officer in a mission to the source of your signal. You'll report to Whele directly within the Service, but you'll be under my operational control and a member of my project staff."

Devron's mind reeled.

Whele added, "The old way was to send senior officers out on these missions, thinking there was some likelihood of a major conflict every time we entered a new solar system. Instead, they'd work—no offense intended—in a billet more suited to a junior officer for a while, come back ages later with some money, and then retire. So now, too many are gone; too many are probably out there doing very little, and too many have come back and retired. My new initiative is to get you younger officers out on projects and let you build some useful experience. It turns out these projects are more about stealth than major space wars anyway.

"If your project gets complicated, you'll have to know when to request assistance. Good judgment is the key. You'll get a salary at the senior space manager's level until the project enters the material recovery phase. You can go back to your civilian job at that point, if you like." Whele looked to Croom, who continued.

"But, for your work on my staff, we'll also offer a contract for lifelong profit sharing at a quarter percent of the total mining proceeds, contingent on successful project completion."

Devron's eyes bulged.

"I see we have your attention," Croom said.

Devron tried to imagine what kind of money that could be, but failed. He was becoming disoriented and fear of failure leapt into his mind. There certainly hadn't been any training to go along with Whele's new initiative. So he didn't fully know what he was being asked to do on this project. "I'm not sure I'm qualified for this."

"We're not sure either, but we'll find out soon enough," Croom said. "Golls are spread thin now. Very thin. With the Argom ships we can lease now, more than a tenth of Whele's officers are currently off into the future. With the time shift for location-shift travel, I mean. And with so many civilians also off-planet, every one of us has to step up. It's as simple as this: you're qualified if you get your job done. Hopefully you know what happens if you don't."

Devron knew.

"But let's start at the beginning. Tell me about your sector and your ship."

Devron sipped his water, focused, and began. "There is no spectral data within the sector indicating metallic resources. But we know such data isn't conclusive. The ship and pilot seem to have performed well. There have been no emergency telemetry reports, so as far as I know, all systems are within normal limits. There were no spurious signal reports before the one of interest. That report seems to describe a valid source, with radio emissions of increasing sophistication. The upgraded interstellar radio exceeded performance expectations and we received the signal report on the first try."

"Devron's ship was only the second to have the upgraded Mark 7C transmitter," said Whele, directing his comment to Croom. "It's the same as the 7B that were sent out on so many ships, just higher input power to the trans-dimension drive. The original Mark 7 was obtained from the Cordans, but the 7A didn't fly on this project. The other ships with the 7C haven't reported yet, so this is its most distant use to date."

"How much higher was the signal strength than predicted, for that distance?" asked Croom, now curious about Devron's knowledge of his ship.

"17%," answered Devron. "The upgrade was to provide better reporting deeper into space. For security purposes, the extra gain won't matter so much, many years from now. But at this point, the data seems to suggest a possible adjustment to the control software."

"Agreed," said Whele.

Devron continued. "I have a draft report prepared for the SSR fleet manager. I'm waiting for the most secret clearance to send it. The extra gain might pose a security risk, even with the highly directional beam."

"Good," commented Croom, thinking Devron might have been a good pick, after all. "Please continue, Devron."

"If I may ask about future use of the trans-dimensional transmitters, when will they be used during these kinds of missions?"

Croom remained motionless, the instinctive Goll reaction to any kind of surprise. "I was about to say you had jumped entirely off topic. But no, maybe you haven't. In a way, that problem does apply to this mission, same as all the others. First, we're not about to give the trans-dimensional radio technology to the Argoms; we stole it fair and square! And we'd have to give them the whole package, from design concepts to materials used, if we tried to take a transmitter onto one of their ships. They examine every piece of our equipment on the manifest, and I won't ever believe it's just for the sake of ships' safety. Also, even if we did give them the technology, how could a trans-dimensional radio's operation be integrated into an Argom gravity-drive ship? I doubt it could ever be done. For our ships with a primitive ion drive, it's a different situation. Apparently someone worked out the math involved."

"I apologize. It does seem off topic."

"Not really. Keep in mind that like all the other missions, when we leave on the Argom ship, we're out there on our own. No communications! We must acknowledge that reality and be prepared."

"Understood." Devron bowed slightly to show his gratitude.

"Good. Reality appropriately acknowledged, preparations to follow. Moving along, what do you know about the 'Old Ones'?"

"Not much. The ship's history file shows my pilot did well in training. Before that, his interface to the ship was completed more quickly than average. His biometric data prior to launch was consistent and he seems to have been structurally sound. But aside from their longevity and reliability, I know little of his race."

Croom looked to Untat and asked, "Would you mind filling in the blanks?" Then he watched Devron.

Untat wished he'd poured a hot drink, but began without delay: "None of us know much about the 'Old Ones.' Quartz clusters with intelligence makes no sense anyway. The Fredans developed the first communications interface thinking they were communicating with distant off-world beings. Idiots! Then they finally realized those radio signals were coming from the interior of their own planet. But that doesn't matter now; it's lost in the past, like the Fredans themselves. Except for the pilots in the ships, the race of the 'Old Ones' is now dead too. After the last of the ships left, the Space Service ordered a project review. It was found the project manager had exceeded his authority for payments to the remaining 'Old Ones.' Worse, the cost and schedule overruns exceeded what would have been needed to develop complete computer control of the ships—"

"Why were computers not used?" asked Devron. "Sorry to interrupt."

"Good question," Untat replied. "That was a very sore subject back in the old days. Some said computers were the only sensible solution. But anyone who thought that was full of biscuits! What computer is as reliable as a solid block of metal-permeated quartz crystal? Not one, even to this minute. That's why the ships' interface units had to be implemented as an array of redundant firmware-based adapters, and not computers, out there on the ships right now."

Devron bowed slightly again.

"Please continue your thoughts about the ships' project manager," said Croom.

"Sorry; I've long been interested in the history of the project and I go off on tangents. Anyway, with the project a total mess financially, he was executed, and all funds paid were ordered seized and recovered. About that time, he and all his voided contracts were fed into an incinerator together. Later, it was found that most of the funds paid to the remaining 'Old Ones' were beyond recovery—by careful design, it seems—and it went from bad to worse. The planet of the 'Old Ones' was ordered destroyed."

Devron was shocked by that, but knew it was important to maintain his composure. And he knew immediately the project review just after the departure of the last ship wasn't a coincidence. The "Old Ones" had been betrayed. But if you play with fire, you get burned. And the "Old Ones," in dealing with the Golls, should have known they were playing with the hottest of fires.

Croom saw no reaction from Devron. Good, he thought. He believed natural grifters were trustworthy, because they were completely predictable.

Untat continued: "So the only possible recovery became just their planet itself. Scientists think there was less supernova activity in this area of the galaxy, maybe much less than elsewhere. Not a lot of metals iron and heavier around here, because they're made only in supernovas. Still, the yield from that planet was enough iron to fill this room, almost as much copper, and more gold and lead than a Goll could possibly carry. And there were aluminum-bearing silicates beyond belief. We'll be running the largest bulk silicate freighters back and forth for years."

"Oh my," interrupted Devron, his composure slipping. He knew some of those silicates had been living beings. Very intelligent living beings. Quickly, he redirected his thoughts. "That would be enough profit to pay for the entire project!"

"Yes," said Croom, liking Devron's apparent reaction. "Many times over. Not only that, we've already replaced all the metals used in the construction of the ships. Do you understand the meaning of the electromagnetic radiation your ship reported?"

"Not fully," Devron replied. "But that kind of radiation is produced with electric current, magnetism, or both. No other methods are known, anyway. So most likely, metals are in use, probably ferrous metals." By beings who don't realize the consequences of what they're doing, he thought. Devron's head spun at another realization. "And if those beings have precious metals at the surface of their planet, where they're least likely to be due to effects of gravity, their entire planet might be permeated, filled entirely with them." Devron reached for his water.

"Exactly," said Croom. "But do you fully understand what's at stake for us?"

"Yes. Unless the source reported by my ship is found to be invalid, and the contracts were then voided, we will be either fantastically rich or fantastically dead." Devron didn't bother to say the obvious: if the report from his ship was invalid, and caused the contracts for a project like this to be voided, he'd be gone immediately.

"It's good not having to waste time explaining the basic concepts," Croom said. "Untat, complete the contracts with Devron and bring them to Whele and me for approvals. Then, Devron and Untat, prepare for the journey to the source. Your checklists will be sent to you. Lift-off is in three days, tenth hour. We've leased an Argom ship, expensive as bribing a minor god, so we can't be late!"

Devron expected the acceleration force to be high on lift-off, but not that high. By the time the Goll shuttle's chemical engines were throttled back, he had long felt uncomfortably trapped in the support box with the Devron-shaped cavity in its padded center.

"I hate this box!" he complained aloud.

But Croom, in the box beside him, had heard. "These modular passenger boxes are confining. They're made only to be easily moved in and out of the shuttles' cargo bays. Not for comfort."

"How long to the ship?"

"Stop complaining and look out that window. There it is now. Marvel at what we've leased, yet again, for so much!"

Devron looked, straining upward in his box to see. The ship was a huge disk with a hole in its center.

"Oh. I thought an Argom ship would be just a larger version of a Goll shuttle."

"No, it's a giant disk. I heard it's built around two circular, counter-rotating particle streams at its core. Altering one stream relative to the other is supposed to provide directional control. The hole in the center is where the gravitational thrust is formed, in the form of a linear graviton jet. It's strong enough to tear the fabric of space and re-form it again to establish the destination. So it can't be used on or near the planet."

"I wish I knew how the interdimensional shift works," thought Devron aloud.

"Me too. The ship itself isn't faster than light, but the end result is the same. Only the Argoms know and they're not telling. That's one of the many advantages of being part of a civilization so old. It makes you wonder what other technologies they have, but aren't leasing out."

As the ship became nearer, Devron saw it wasn't a flat disk, as it had appeared initially. It had a great thickness, indicating massive structural strength. The transition between the enormous engine and the outer edges of the disk became apparent.

Croom noticed that too. "The quarters, cargo bays, and crew spaces are in the circular fairing, the outer portion of the disk. The fairing has its own two pairs of smaller particle streams, for inertial stabilization. Meaning we won't be crushed when they start the engine."

Devron watched the Argom ship get larger still, with it gradually going out of view from his window as the shuttle arced toward it. "It must be huge," he observed. "Its mass must— That's odd; I just thought—"

"Shut up. Don't say it. A word?"

"Yes!"

"Don't ever say it," Croom ordered.

"But it's nonsense!"

"Doesn't matter. It's from the ship. I thought it too. We're not sure what it comes from, but maybe it's the gravity streams at idle power. But we're not going to let the Argoms know we hear their ships. Understood?"

"Yes."

"Anyway, I think it just means the ship is idling and ready to go."

Devron marveled at the massive power of the now-unseen ship. Having a gravity thruster powerful enough to rip and re-form space-time was one thing. But <u>feeling</u> it ready to go, with its nonsensical one-word statement clear in his mind, was far more impressive.

"Calm down," said Croom. "It's just transportation. You'd better focus on what we need to do when we get there."

His pre-launch preparation checklists now seemed trivial and ludicrously inadequate. I have no idea what I'm supposed to do there, Devron concluded. The thought was anything but calming.

After reporting aboard, Devron was shown into his small quarters, Room 6. As he entered, lighting came up and an automated welcome and safety briefing began on the room's monitor. The briefing was a mechanical-sounding translation to Goll and strangely predictable. Even boring. So Devron's attention drifted to the contents of the room.

The room itself had obviously been machined from some enormous block of metal, and its strength seemed to be immense. The floor had a solidity that Devron had never experienced before, making it now clear that the outer corridor walkway's removable grating wasn't intended to be as load bearing, in comparison.

A modular Goll-shaped chair, obviously installed for him, was in the center of the room. It seemed to be adjustable for both work and rest and it was positioned for him to face the monitor panel. Its side supports had identical Goll-language labeled control panels, with keys suitable for his gripper nails. He placed his two travel bags into a latching bin located under a small tabletop.

The automated briefing ended abruptly and was replaced by a more urgent-sounding message: "Passengers, please take your places in the chairs provided! Recline your chair to its flattest position. Pull the restraint net upward from its container, stretch it over your thorax segments, and attach it to the buckles on the opposite side support of your chair. Attachment is remotely monitored and all passengers must be restrained before the mission can begin! Press the 'Request assistance' button on your control if assistance is required!"

Devron rushed to the chair, sat into it, folded his appendages, and reclined. The chair didn't go completely flat, so the monitor was still visible. Devron started fussing with the restraint net. It seemed poorly suited for a Goll, even though the chair itself was comfortable. The net snagged on all the barbs on the edges of his arms and was intensely annoying. He dreaded delaying the mission, but finally he had himself buckled in.

Almost immediately, a schematic image of the ship appeared on the monitor, with the announcement: "Particle beam phasing checks!"

So I was last to get my net buckled, Devron thought with slight embarrassment. Red and green undulating rings were shown at the center of the schematic diagram and the room seemed to reel accordingly. At first, Devron couldn't tell if the room was actually moving or if only the vestibular system in his thorax was being affected. But when he considered the massive rigidity of the room again, the latter seemed more likely.

"Fairing inertial dampening checks!" The schematic on the monitor then showed multi-colored wavy lines at the inner and outer edges of the ship's disk, outboard from the engine. The room seemed to sway again.

The schematic went blank again. "Preflight checks complete! Passengers may choose to activate their overhead displays by selecting the 'Overhead monitor' key on your seat control panels."

Devron located and pressed that key on the right-side panel. With a slight flicker, the entire overhead changed from a view of machined metal with an odd crystalline texture to one of all the stars in space. The result was extremely impressive.

Then the flight began with only a brief announcement: "Engaging engine." The entire room went rubbery, with the inertial stabilization tuning to synchronize with the engine. The loud droning of the engine, emanating from every surface in the room, even the ceiling display, increased in both frequency and volume.

The stars overhead moved slowly at first, with only the ones near the center converging slowly. Then, with an increasing rush, all of the universe seemed to be suddenly sucked to the side, toward the engine intake. A wave of panic rushed through Devron with the sudden darkness and he was completely immobile.

"It's only photons arrived here from distant stars, gathered into a lens of torn space!" he said to himself, but the mild panic of seeing the universe ripped into the engine remained.

"It's only photons arrived here from distant stars, gathered into a lens of torn space!" Devron repeated, with urgency.

"Quarters room 6, do you require assistance?" came from the monitor speaker.

"No!" answered Devron, louder than he had intended. By the Infernal Grandmother of All The Gods, he hadn't known his quarters were monitored for sound! Or had that been covered in the automated briefing?

The engine's droning diminished and then the universe gushed out across the ceiling, apparently reborn again. But the stars were obviously different.

The Argom pilot approached the source carefully.

The ship's three navigators, all software entities within the ship's computer, had planned a tangential reformation burst relative to the source solar system, with a long offset from its ecliptic. By doing so, the intense graviton jet from the engine, produced while the ship emerged into this space, would be directed well away from any likely detection point.

As the ship entered the destination space, the Argom pilot on duty watched his helmet chart display as sensors populated symbols within it for planets, moons, debris, and tactical information. Tactical symbols, scores of them, were concentrated around the third planet. The volume of data was large and quickly growing. The pilot had to continually declutter his display image around the third planet, as more and more information came in.

Then one large moon was displayed. The pilot zoomed in his helmet display to the third planet and its moon, watching the moon especially. There were no tactical symbols shown for the moon. The pilot watched and waited, occasionally decluttering tactical info from the planet. There was still no tactical data from the moon! No radio emissions, no artificial heat signatures, no artificial lights, and no artificial spectral signatures. So if there were defense facilities built into the moon, they were carefully masked.

But then the pilot knew that with every possible kind of noise coming from the third planet, those fools weren't the careful type. So he put his cursor over the moon's icon and manually entered "Uninhabited, undefended, and undeveloped, despite being so close." The cursed Golls will like that, the pilot thought.

With no system-level defenses to be concerned about, and none at all on the moon, the pilot became curious about other data. He zoomed back out to the entire system, moved his cursor over "Display," then "Mass Properties," then "Spectral Analysis."

On his display, the tactical data still growing around the third planet disappeared, and much of the area inside the large fifth planet erupted into bright colors. Shades of red were predominant.

"I'm rich!" the pilot shouted, very uncharac- teristically.

Devron found a place at the conference room table and plopped his lower thorax onto the floor. The flight itself had been disconcerting, but today all he felt was stress about the project's first staff meeting at the destination. Croom was right; one can't be distracted by the transportation.

Devron had studied the Space Service's manuals from the outset, and prepared careful notes. His high-level plan, formed while preparing for the mission:

- Identify solar system physical configuration.
- Evaluate the system for possible sensor systems which might detect us—perform again with every following step.

- Set up external security for the operation, maybe with passive probes to detect arrival of other spacecraft.
- Launch and upload data from the initial probe.
- Identify defense characteristics of the source planet.
- Identify masked areas where an initial operating base might be established.
- Set up the first operating base.
- Probe closer to the source and obtain complete data on the source planet.
- Form a plan to defeat planetary defenses.
- Attack and take control of the planet.

Maybe that would suffice, amateurish as the others might think it was. The first probe was already underway, with Croom's permission. But now, with the deluge of data coming in, he wasn't sure what to think. He logged into a monitor in the conference table's surface and opened his notes.

"Everyone ready to begin?" Croom asked loudly.

The conference room became silent.

Croom sipped the hot water he seemed to always have in meetings, then began. "Anyone in their feeding cycle?" All Golls in the room but Croom and Untat raised both their topmost arms. "Well, that was sudden. Hopefully involuntary excretions during that accursed flight aren't to blame! Untat, pass a bale of biscuits to the table, please."

Soon every Goll but two had a biscuit end protruding from his maw.

"I realize this thing's been hurried and chaotic. There's sure to be more chaos before it's all done. But I ask you all to remain focused within your assigned areas and keep me informed. Speaking of focus, I know you've all seen the data coming in about the metallic resources. I don't want to hear about that. We're going to run this thing like we have to take every precaution, and work very hard, for not enough metal to fill this cup. Understand? Bad news, especially, I need to hear right away. Untat, do you have an opening statement?"

"No."

"Does anyone else have any questions or comments before we begin?"

There were none.

Croom continued. "Good. Or maybe you're just too focused on your biscuits. But right now, the ship is in the destination space and it's being maneuvered toward the system disk. It's a very flat system, but don't start thinking in just two dimensions. Threats could be anywhere. The Argom's report shows—if you can believe this—nothing about system defenses, just all kinds of noise from the third planet. But I want you to be on guard for the unexpected. I don't want to get ambushed while we're figuring out how to take the planet."

Croom sipped his hot drink with the usual unhurried pause. "So far, I like how the Argoms have approached the system and their reports are good. Now it's time for us to take charge and let the Argoms know where we're going to set up. They'll need to know that soon. Devron, what do you have?"

Devron pulled his biscuit from his maw using the gripper of his left midarm. "Our first probe has entered initial orbit around the third planet already. With its recon algorithm carefully set for threats, being so close is a clear indication that defensive and sensing systems are weak. Passive sensors are a possibility, with so many strong emissions from the planet. But I don't think anyone is listening. All the defense and communications systems we've detected so far are wide-angle emissions, even if they're directional at all. So it's just full-spectrum radio-frequency noise blaring everywhere. I trust our probe more than the Argom's, but all our data correlates with theirs."

"So what threats are there to this ship and our operations?"

Devron knew he was on a hot spot. "None detected so far, it seems. Nothing."

"What about the planet itself? How hardened is it?"

"Not at all. Everything is out in the open, right on the surface. Major cities are built next to large bodies of water. The smallest disruptions to the planet would cause the water to destroy those cities entirely."

"There are no underground systems?"

"None, except for some material mining. Not any significant depth, even then. It's amazing!"

Croom was beyond amazed. What race of people would live like this? Being completely out in the open, sitting on top of an immense treasure of precious metals, transmitting their noise all across the galaxy, inviting anyone to come get it! Just the thought of it was chilling. "Recommendations?"

"The policy manuals I've been reading say to mask farther out. Maybe within the outer ecliptic dust, too far from the star for planet formation. In this situation, with so much debris orbiting between the fourth and fifth planets, I recommend we set up there. It's still a long way from the third planet, relative to their undeveloped moon. But closer for us to send in the next sets of probes."

"Good!" Croom looked uncharacteristically pleased for an instant. "Well, Devron's lucky. This might turn out to be a vacation trip for him." Croom grimaced as he saw Devron's biscuit go back into his maw, and begin to move side to side, being worked by his mandibles. "With a free dinner." Croom sipped, and his countenance resumed his usual appearance of general concern. "But all those RF transmissions have to have some importance. Maybe we're missing something big. Rok, what do you have so far?"

Rok, the data systems manager, was next to withdraw his biscuit. But he looked like he was having trouble deciding what to say. After an uncomfortable pause, he blurted out, "Video transmissions for various games, played with different kinds of small objects, each referred to as a 'ball.' Weather forecasting based on the behavior of a small, apparently useless, digging animal. Exhortations to buy drinks containing ethyl alcohol, which causes both acute and chronic disease, then causes the beings to wreck their vehicles and kill themselves—"

"Hold it right there, Rok," Croom interrupted.

Devron felt sickened, in a way he hadn't felt before. He put his partially eaten biscuit on the table.

Rok continued anyway, with greatly increasing volume. "Discussions about unpleasant odors from genitalia, itching genitalia, skin wrinkles—"

"Rok! We don't have time for nonsense. I won't allow this—"

"Video transmissions of disputed sexual paternity. Endless audio transmissions of random sound vibrations. And are you ready for this?! They use cut-up parts of living things to build their structures! And even for the furnishings they rest and work upon! I'm as serious as a hull breach! It's insane!"

The conference room was abruptly quiet, except for biscuits being placed on the table or dropping onto the floor.

Rok was obviously struggling to regain his composure. His antennae oddly bounced and twitched simultaneously.

Croom continued with a voice that was calm, but forced. "Let's stop, then take this one step at a time. So the probe has worked out language translation, or what it thinks is a language translation. Are we sure the translation process didn't—"

Devron's monitor flashed red and text streamed across the top. "Croom! Our probe has been destroyed!"

Croom leaned back, shifting weight to his hindlegs. "Let's stay calm. It was just a small machine, one of many probes we have. Devron, your vacation's canceled. Find out what happened to that probe and send me a detailed report, quickly. Untat, tell the Argoms to mask behind the debris belt Devron described. No more probes are to be launched until we know what happened to the first one. All the rest of you, let's proceed under the assumption the probe was destroyed by a defensive system we haven't detected yet, and let's be careful. Send me a report containing anything of interest, as necessary.

Rok, I want a detailed briefing about your data, with Untat in attendance. Call us both after you've composed yourself and prepared a proper briefing. I'm sorry to be so abrupt, but meeting adjourned!"

A short time later, working in his quarters, Devron discovered the probe had been destroyed by a piece of space junk. The probe had suddenly transmitted a burst of proximity alarms, dozens of them, then hundreds, and then had presumably been destroyed in a collision. He then queried the Argoms and the massive amount of debris in orbit around the third planet became fully clear.

He prepared a report, proofread it twice, and sent it to Croom and Untat. Devron knew the call back wouldn't take long. He was right.

"Croom here. I need to be sure I understand this. They've left pieces of debris, by the hundreds of thousands, orbiting their own home world?"

"Yes. There's no doubt. Maybe millions."

"Incredible. I would have never thought anyone would do that, even around an enemy's planet."

Devron knew Croom had stored away a new dirty trick for future use. "The software engineers who programmed the probes apparently didn't think of it either."

"Devron, those idiots on that planet are dangerous. They're dangerous to our equipment, maybe without being smart enough to create real defenses. And they're dangerous to our people." Croom paused, his mind obviously reeling.

Devron then assumed Croom had already received Rok's briefing, but decided not to say anything about that.

"You know what this means?" Croom asked.

"Yes, I think I do. It won't be safe to use shuttles around the planet. So we can't mine it from its surface, in the conventional sense. But it's mostly a chunk of iron, with a huge core of precious metals. The whole thing needs to be processed anyway."

"Exactly. I want it blown to pieces, the smaller the better. We just need to keep the debris belt somewhere near the planet's current orbit. Then all of it could be recovered using bulk processing ships, without having to chase pieces everywhere. They're designed for that kind of thing. It'll then be safe to mine the rest of this system too. We can legally lay claim to it all after those idiots cease to exist."

Devron thought for a moment, then said, "The directed-energy weapons we have can't destroy it from this distance. Everything else depends on delivering something to the planet, or delivery, retrieval, and delivery again. The kits for synthesizing chemical or biological weapons require sampling from on-planet probes and then analysis in the lab kit. We have three kinds of fusion weapons, but they could be damaged in the debris field, or maybe even intercepted."

"Then find some other solution. I'm calling another staff meeting tomorrow, eighth hour. Maybe we can get all the way through a meeting this time. Out."

Rok spoke up at the beginning of the next meeting. "I apologize for my conduct yesterday. Reviewing the transmissions from that nasty planet was difficult for me. Very difficult—"

"Thank you," interrupted Croom. "Rok's data is unbelievably disturbing. So I simply cannot allow any one of you, or myself, to dwell on it. In all of the history of Goll travels, conquests, and gathering of alien technologies, there have been no reports of such extreme depravity and mass stupidity. But that hardly begins to describe—" Croom struggled for words. "But I cannot, and will not describe it. We cannot bear it. So I ask that we accept that the complete destruction of the vile inhabitants of that planet is a wholly good and necessary outcome. Let's proceed accordingly."

Croom sipped his hot water and continued. "As all of you in the meeting have noticed, I want a solution for destroying that planet from a stand-off distance, as far away as possible. Who has something?"

Croom looked to Devron, but Rok spoke up again. "This is an information problem. So yesterday I developed algorithms to search all the data we're getting from the planet. I've been using them since then, and I found how <u>they</u> imagine their planet would be destroyed."

"Really," Croom said, not really asking, and not really surprised. He knew now that anything could come from that insane planet.

"They have produced videos describing how large pieces of debris, originating within the solar system, could blow the planet to bits. The videos show the certain destruction being avoided in various implausible ways. But they know it could happen."

"Devron, what do you think?"

"Same as yesterday: the weapons we have in the mission kits won't get the job done, with certainty, from a safe distance. We know the probes are vulnerable to their orbiting debris. So if we want to track their debris field, we'd have to move this ship in closer, and we'd be detected. I'm sure of it. Scanning for debris would be as noticeable as shining around light from a second star. Then, having exposed ourselves, we'd be open to any kind of attack they could think of. Very dangerous, very unpredictable."

"Agreed."

"Even if we talked the Argoms into moving their ship close enough to hit the planet with their gravity drive, which they won't do, they could blow metals half way across the galaxy with this thing. Or worse, straight into some other dimension. Impractical, maybe impossible, to control the results."

Croom thought a while. The others waited. "So how do we do this?"

"There are remote-controlled thrusters in one of the mission kits, four big ones," Rok said. "I checked. With gimbal mounts too, but they're designed to mount onto flat surfaces."

"There is equipment for processing iron too, isn't there?" asked Devron.

"Yes," answered Rok. "But I don't know anything about it."

"Shortest meetings I've ever had," said Croom. "Devron, you're transferred back to manufacturing early. Figure out how to get those thrusters mounted to one of these big rocks. Design and make anything you need to make it happen. Rok, figuring the trajectory to that planet is an information problem too. So you're on it. Report all your problems to Untat; report your solutions to me. Any questions?"

"Yes," Devron said. "The densest pieces in this belt of debris are almost pure nickel-iron. As a projectile, we'd want to use the biggest, densest piece we could move with an acceptable velocity vector. But the velocity's going to be very high at the planet anyway—"

"So what's your question?"

"Do you mind if we use a giant piece of iron as a bullet?"

"What do I care, as long as you turn that planet inside out?"

"It'll be expensive."

"No, it won't. Let's just assume all the pieces of your Big Iron Bullet will be recovered along with the pieces of that planet. Even if they aren't, I don't care. Get it done. Any more questions?"

"Yes," said Rok.

"So much for short meetings!"

"Can I talk to the Argoms about this?"

"Yes. Thanks for the reminder." Croom bowed toward Rok. "Another item I didn't take the time to mention: the Argom ship is quarantined here until this project is done. They can maneuver their ship within the system, but we are not to produce any electromagnetic emissions and we may not leave this solar system for any reason. That's my interpretation from the policy manual, and I've informed the Argom crew. Any more questions?"

There weren't any.

"Meeting adjourned. Let's have another dysfunctional, off-the-agenda meeting same time tomorrow. Get to work!"

"Now what?" asked Croom as soon as he'd entered the conference room, passing Devron on his way to the hot water carafe.

Devron looked at Rok, then to Croom, and began: "We have a new idea. But first, I'd like to tell you how we came to it."

"Be brief in describing what doesn't work."

"We have the thrusters and we have the mounts. But we'd definitely need adapters between the mounts and the Big Iron Bullet. It's not practical to create a flat side on such a large piece of nickel-iron with the equipment we have, or maybe with any equipment. So suppose just four interface adapters could be made. We have a processing machine which could be used to create molten iron for iron castings. But we don't have any materials for proper molds. We could try making forms from silicates from the non-ferrous pieces of debris, but it would be tricky. None of us has any experience molding large amounts of iron. Getting the molten iron into the forms in a low-gravity field would be risky anyway. In any case, the thrust generated would be very little for the kind of mass we want. Both acceleration and control would be minimal. So there's more risk, of every kind, with so much time needed to get it to the planet."

"So what does work?"

Rok took up the tale: "I talked to the Argoms. We think we could use the ship's engine to shoot the Big Iron Bullet."

"Wait. If it would shoot metal out of the system, and make the big mess we talked about, how is this acceptable?"

"That was to be done by applying the gravity drive directly to the planet, intentionally strong enough to blow it apart. This is different. If we apply a controlled force to a smaller piece of solid iron—smaller than the planet, I mean—it would accelerate away before disintegrating. They have a space-dockyard maneuvering mode, which limits engine output."

"So the Big Iron Bullet would accelerate very quickly, but with relatively low internal stresses," added Devron.

"I get the concept," said Croom, with slight impatience. "Are the Argoms willing to do this?"

"A pilot is waiting for us right now in the control room," said Rok. "They have a huge piece of nickel-iron picked out. They say a targeting solution has been found for it, which will minimize material loss. But only three of us will fit in there with the pilot."

Croom decided to proceed. "Untat, work with the rest of the staff to monitor the planet and maintain security. Rok and Devron, come with me."

The control room was small, even for the Argom pilot. With three Golls, it was cramped. The Golls were gathered tightly together, not wanting to touch any of the controls around the perimeter of the room.

Devron saw the truth of it instantly. The Argoms saw every other room in the ship's fairing as a revenue-generating facility. Even the spacious conference room they'd been using must have been designed under that assumption. So this control room, having no revenue potential, was kept as small as possible.

The Argom pilot was seated in his control chair and was wearing a full-coverage helmet over his massive head. He had no control panel, but a large display panel on a side wall was active. Devron assumed it was only for their benefit.

A monotone voice came out of a speaker on the overhead, translated to Goll: "Welcome, Golls. I will dispense with preliminaries. Do you now wish to launch an asteroid toward the third planet, to destroy it?"

Croom looked to Devron. Devron said, "This is our best option. I recommend we proceed."

Croom turned to the pilot and said, "Do it."

"Agreed and recorded," answered the pilot. "I am maneuvering not to the selected object, but to an initial point calculated by the flight director, in space-dockyard thruster mode. From there, the ship will move toward the object, then stop near it. While the ship is decelerating, a small gravity beam will be produced, which will strike the object.

"Do not be alarmed by sudden motions. The control script I have prepared uses the ship's standard control laws which will maintain a safe distance from the object and other hazards. I have also written custom control laws to limit the forces applied to the object, which should prevent it from fracturing. As in the other ship's spaces you've been using, this area has inertial stabilization, so you will not feel the acceleration or deceleration of the ship.

"The script is repetitive. Expect multiple approaches to the object. After each approach, the computed trajectory will be displayed on this screen.

"The target has a thin basaltic crust over its nickel-iron material and other loose debris adheres to it due to its gravity field. Those materials will be swept aside at the end of the first approach.

"The first approach will begin now."

The monitor showed sudden movement and a dot appeared in the center of the monitor. It grew larger with amazing quickness.

"Oh!" said Rok, without meaning to, and locked into involuntary immobility, as did the other Golls, expecting an immediate crash into the gigantic iron mountain. But the ship had already stopped; the amazed Golls were slow to perceive they were indeed motionless. The nearest surface of the iron mountain range glowed red just as suddenly as the ship had stopped. Molten bits of debris flew away radially, disappearing off all edges of the monitor.

"Do not be alarmed by sudden motions," repeated the pilot.

"I <u>was</u> alarmed," said Rok. "I'll be alarmed next time, too!"

"Unbelievable!" gasped Croom.

"Do the molten pieces being ejected affect the trajectory?" asked Devron.

"Yes, but minimally. The computer will recalculate the target solution based only on mass of the remaining material and the flight director script will be updated," said the pilot. "Also, observe the gravity impulse was sufficient to not only stop the ship, but to back away slightly. The trajectory to the target planet is displayed now." And it was. It showed a clean miss of the planet in a little more than three years. "The next approach is already underway. The ship will be backed away slowly to simplify computations."

Devron thought of another question: "We're heating the object. Will there be a noticeable infrared signature?"

"Very slight. On the side toward the target planet, almost none. The object is very massive, and most heat will be radiated to open space, away from the planet."

The next approach happened in a little more than two hours. It resulted in a closer miss, in 2.6 years. All three Golls were again alarmed by sudden motions.

Croom asked, "How much time will be required to complete the script?"

"Probably three standard days."

"Good. Thank you both for the impressive flying and for demonstrating the script to us. We will leave you to your work. May we rejoin you in three days?"

"Yes, you are welcome here at any time. I will brief the relief pilots as necessary. You will be informed when the script nears completion."

"Thank you again."

The Golls left the control room and stopped in the ship's main, circular hallway.

"That was as much of that as I could take!" Croom said.

"Me too," said Rok. "I'll see you in three days. Forget their chair; I need to go curl up in a dark corner!"

Three days later, the three Golls were back in the control room.

The approaches to the Big Iron Bullet were not quite so close and much easier to watch.

"Adjustments to trajectory are more minor at this point in the script," a different pilot said. "Observe the displayed trajectory."

The monitor showed impact almost exactly centered on the planet, in ninety-one days.

The pilot said, "Only one more approach should be needed."

Two hours later, the Big Iron Bullet was on its way, with eighty-six days to impact.

"This trajectory, together with the object's mass, will almost certainly result in an impact," said the pilot. "The object's momentum is very high and no known mechanism from the target planet would be sufficient to deflect it away. And they seem to have no method of destroying so much mass."

"Good," said Croom. "Has the script affected the ship?"

"The ship remains fully operational," said the pilot.

"Again, thank you for your work in this effort. Your assistance and efficiency will be recorded. Please pass my sincere thanks to all the other pilots. We will return to our quarters now."

In the main hallway, they stopped in the same place as before.

"So, the waiting begins. I ask that you remain patient. Let's meet every five days for status reports. Rok, assemble all your data and set up a secure archive for all the information we've received from that planet. I'll have Untat organize a review of the archive; but Devron, you'll have responsibility for military information. If there's anything that could be useful to Golls in the future, now's the time to store it away." Croom turned and walked toward his quarters.

Devron turned to Rok. "I expect military action from the target planet. I'm not overly concerned about damage to the Big Iron Bullet. I agree with the Argom pilot; they can't destroy it or deflect it enough to miss. But we have to assume they'll try something. Please monitor their transmissions for any sign of a response and inform me immediately."

"I will," said Rok.

Twelve meetings later, Rok presented his analysis of the planet's planned attack on the Big Iron Bullet.

"Rockets are being prepared for launch tomorrow, soon after our tenth hour. There has been a concentrated, hurried program to prepare as many rockets as possible. I expect a mass launch of twenty to twenty-four rockets, depending on how many are operable at that time.

"The rockets are armed with lithium deuteride fusion weapons. They have the advantages of simplicity, light weight and high yield. Light weight is important because the rockets are being used far beyond their originally designed ranges, and throw weight becomes critical."

Devron hadn't realized it until just then, but Rok had become more detached from the people on the planet. He thought that was a good thing.

Croom asked the obvious question first. "What effect do you expect these weapons to have?"

"Overall, none," Rok replied. "Their plan is to detonate the weapons to one side of the object. It's been announced on the planet that enough force might be applied to divert the object away. But that is clearly not so. My calculations show only a slight yawing motion will result and a minor amount of debris will be ejected. The effect on the object's trajectory will be negligible.

Even most of the ejected debris will still strike the planet, near the asteroid's point of impact."

"They're proficient with mathematics. Otherwise they wouldn't have rockets or fusion weapons. Do you believe they somehow miscalculated the result?"

"No. The weapon and rocket programs seem to be a true maximum effort. But it's clear the effect is being miscommunicated to the populace for control of panic. Those people can't face the reality of their mortality, even at the end of a normal lifespan. So a major crisis such as this can turn them into herds of insane fiends and complete destruction of their society can result. And that will almost certainly happen anyway."

"That's disgusting!"

Devron agreed, but silently. He was glad that Rok was making the presentation. He wasn't sure how to articulate his revulsion, or whether he should. He had never before considered the end of a society through uncontrolled panic.

Croom was silent only a moment. "I've never been so sure I was doing the right thing. I won't call a meeting tomorrow for their charade. View it on your monitors, if you care to. If there's any result of significance, we'll discuss it during the next regular meeting, five days from now."

Croom stood and walked out of the conference room.

✦ ✦ ✦

At the fifth hour on the eighty-sixth day, the Golls met in the usual conference room. An audio feed was provided to and from the ship's pilot in the control room.

"Greetings, Golls," the pilot said.

"Greetings," said Croom.

"The object will strike the planet in the time shown on your monitors."

The monitors in the conference room table top showed the planet with remarkable resolution and clarity. Devron could see glowing spots on the dark side, which he already knew were burning cities. But he was far beyond any sympathy. The upper right corner in each showed a time counting down from about eighteen minutes.

The Golls waited silently. Hot water was sipped and Untat consumed his biscuit.

Finally, the Big Iron Bullet came into the display with incredible speed; in less than a second it struck the planet with a small flash of light and a huge explosion. The display zoomed outward to show the growing cloud of dust. The planet was gone. The closer half of the planet's moon had been blown away from a glancing collision and the remaining portion was slowly spinning and collapsing into a ball of rubble.

The power of the collision was incredible. The Golls watched silently as the display continued to zoom outward. Devron wondered how much material had been ejected beyond recovery but kept his thoughts to himself.

"Thank you," Croom finally said to the pilot. "This project is now in the property claim phase. So I claim this system as property of the Goll Empire, to be governed by our project officers until the system is formally handed off for recovery. You have all been very helpful. I will include commendations for you and the other pilots in my report. Normally, an increase in share results, but I cannot guarantee that. Please return us to Goll."

"Acknowledged," said the pilot. "And recorded. The checklist for the return journey will be activated. Expect departure in about six hours to allow for clearing maneuvers."

"Thank you," said Croom. "You may terminate the video and audio feed to this room."

Croom looked around the room. "Thank you, gentlemen. Untat, we have claim paperwork to prepare. Soon you all will be rich. But there is something more important to consider: we have removed an infection of extreme ignorance and insanity from the galaxy. So all life forms within it are now healthier and stronger. Thank you all for that beneficial result."

"Thank you," said Untat, then each of the others followed suit.

"If you get bored in the easy life, let me know. There's more work to do." With that, Croom stood and walked from the room.

Devron considered his quarter percentage. Even his share could turn out to be more heavy metals than had ever been known to the Golls. The entire financial system of the Golls might have to be reinvented by the time this system was fully processed.

He wondered whether he'd live to enjoy his immense wealth. But as he walked to his quarters, his mind was at ease. He knew, either way, all his worries would soon be coming to an end.

RAIN OF DEATH

If I describe how the next story originated at this point, I'd almost certainly give away too much. So, after reading the story, please see the epilogue which follows.

✦ ✦ ✦

With a small splash, a human hand fell into the water, near the entrance corner of the lower rice paddy. Ng Li sighed and looked sideward at the hand. The rings of paddy water spreading from the still-bobbing hand seemed to propagate filth through the field. Li refocused on her work and finished planting the rice shoots into the final row of the paddy. While she worked, Li's dislike of having the severed hand in her freshly planted paddy grew steadily.

When she finished the planting, Li stood upright and stretched her sore back slowly, still sweating freely in the warm drizzle falling from the always-cloudy sky. New Shanghai was a hot, wet planet and still an under-developed colony. Bamboo brought from Earth was thriving in the new forests; the hardwood trees were not. Rice grew well, but was planted and harvested only manually, in too few paddies. There wasn't yet enough equipment for development of the planned croplands, or for adequate rice production in the existing croplands. And, as Li knew only too well, there weren't enough farmers for this labor-intensive kind of farming. After the 100 kilos of rice were paid for her annual taxes, there was barely enough rice to survive until the next year. Except for bamboo, the only thing in abundance were the deadly native snakes, which defied every attempt at eradication.

After twisting left and right to ease the last knots in her back, Li waded over to observe the hand more closely. It was now motionless, floating palm upward. It was a man's hand, without dirt or callouses. It had been cleanly cut through the wrist, apparently by something extremely powerful and sharp. Not wanting to touch it directly, she scooped up the hand using her rice-shoot basket. She tilted the basket to flip the hand over, and checked it again.

The hand was lightly tanned, except for a lighter band on the little finger, where a ring must have been removed. Its nails were manicured perfectly and seemed smooth and nicely shaped. Li glanced at her thumbs at the edge of the basket, seeing them as worn, ragged, water-soaked, and filthy in comparison.

Enough, she thought, and walked to the corner of the paddy, where four partially buried bamboo logs formed two steps upward to the edge of the terrace. Up onto the path on top of the lower terrace, she began her walk through the lushly green, shin-high grass to her lonely hut. As she walked, she gradually wiped mud from her lower legs and feet into the wet grass.

With the rice planted, it was time to cut the grass along this path again, she thought. It would keep the snakes away. She intensely hated snakes near her hut or paddies. Every snake she saw was quickly but carefully killed with the stout length of bamboo she always wore across her back. Almost as quickly, their foul-smelling meat was cooked and eaten before it spoiled in the heat.

Her back was very sore and she knew cutting grass would be difficult with her short-handled sickle. She would do that the day after tomorrow, she decided. The roof of her hut and the pig pen fence needed to be repaired first; those tasks would give her back a day to recover.

As with all body parts, she knew the hand would be a welcome treat for the pigs, which otherwise ate mostly bamboo shoots, ferns, and young leaves. And hands weren't too hard to divide. She would make two cuts from finger webs to the wrist joint: between the first and middle fingers, and on the other side of the middle finger. Then, cutting the hand from the stub of the wrist would yield four pieces for the four pigs.

Some parts were easier to divide, some harder. Leg pieces were usually fed as three parts flesh, one part bone. Portions of abdomen and gut were easy to cut up, but nasty; shoulders and ribs difficult, but usually not so filthy. She never tried to divide heads, or pieces of heads; the pigs would always have to fight over those.

She hadn't liked giving body parts to her mother's pigs when she was a girl. She had worried that the pigs would learn to enjoy human flesh and they would eventually attack her. But as she matured, she came to understand that pigs saw her only as the provider, and their welcoming grunts as she approached the pig pen became less ominous. And with God providing body parts, how could they be useful, other than feeding them to pigs?

Her mother said the fallen parts were sometimes cooked and eaten by the villagers, but she would never consider doing such a thing. The bitter snake meat was her only protein. Her pigs were sold in the village, where so much pork could be sold and eaten before it spoiled.

She would love to eat pork regularly, like the wealthy villagers did. Her envy flared. The corrupt, wicked villagers had easier lives. But most troubling, there were rumors of a growing black magic cult spreading among the villages. So she would never marry a villager, she promised herself again, even though farmers became fewer and poorer.

Something suddenly hit the left edge of her conical hat and rolled off, in a snake-like way. She jumped away from it instinctively, dropping the hand from her basket. But it wasn't a snake; it was a length of large intestine. Some filth was emerging from one of the bloody ends.

Some tears came to her eyes and she held the back of her dirty left hand to her mouth, as if she were warding away the piece of gut. "God, why do you do this?" she wondered aloud, with a sob. But she knew she was being weak, as her mother had so often accused.

Li regained some composure, checked the grass for snakes, walked to the edge of the upper paddy, and sat at its edge. She took off her rice-straw hat, and as she expected, saw both blood and filth in one smudged spot. She put the dirty edge into the paddy water, and soaked that part of her hat in the clear, undisturbed water for a few minutes. Then she waved the hat gently, still in the water, to rinse away the mess. She checked the hat, and soaked it again. After the second time, only a slight discoloration remained.

She replaced her hat, stood, and walked back to scoop the two body parts up into her basket. Her mother would not approve of her attitude, she knew. She would remind Li that God provided essential food for the pigs, and that her lack of gratitude was sinful. And that she brought shame upon the family with her weaknesses. And that she was such a disappointment, and would never find a husband. And that she wished she had given birth to a son instead. And that Li's father wept in the afterlife, seeing that he'd left behind such a pathetic child.

Li wept openly as she slowly walked to her hut.

Ohn Ben, Ng Li's great-uncle she'd never met, walked meekly into the castle's courtroom, and two hooded doormen closed the strong doors behind him. His bare feet made no sound on the cold stone floor, worn smooth by bare feet beyond counting. As he had been instructed, he removed all his clothing and placed it into the worn basket beyond the door. He pulled a large signet ring from the middle finger of his left hand, then dropped it onto his worn clothing. Then, with silent anguish, he gently removed his dead wife's ring from the little finger of the same hand. He bent and placed her ring beside his, with reverence.

Naked and shivering, he walked around the basket, toward the sword floating in the air, well above his height. As he approached the sword, it began to glow a dull red.

Ohn Ben lowered himself to his knees in the appointed place, within the black square painted on the floor. He bowed forward until his forehead touched the floor. Without rising, he said, "Lord Shimi, please judge my sins!"

A blackness without form swirled into the fabric of a dark robe and suddenly, Lord Shimi was standing in front of Ohn Ben. The glowing sword hung between them. Lord Shimi regarded the prostrate form with disgust and said in a deep, booming voice, "Rise, you swine!"

Ohn Ben rose, careful to keep his eyes downward.

"Extend both your arms, thief!"

Ohn Ben's arms shook as they rose, but remained more still once extended.

"The Arabs, filth that they were, devised a fair punishment for thieves." The dark castle boomed with Lord Shimi's voice. "THEY TAKE THEIR HANDS!"

Almost too fast to be seen, with a sharp slash, the sword took away Ohn Ben's left hand in a flash of red light.

Ohn Ben gasped and tears dripped off his down-turned face. But he remained almost still.

Lord Shimi laughed. "My sword seems to believe your crime was worth only one hand!"

With another loud whistle, the sword took Ohn Ben's other hand, and it seemed to fly through the stone ceiling. He moaned in pain.

"Well! It seems you were more guilty than I first thought," Lord Shimi laughed. "Don't worry. Both your hands are out there somewhere in my lands, fattening pigs or maybe feeding insects!"

Ohn Ben slowly raised his head and looked directly into Lord Shimi's eyes with defiance.

Lord Shimi saw the defiant look and laughed in delight. Ohn Ben was suddenly snatched upward by an unseen force, as though invisible hands pulled his arms and legs painfully apart. The flashing sword chopped Ohn Ben to bits, with the sound of a whirring whirlwind. Each piece seemed to be flung away, without blood, with only one sharp shriek.

"Good riddance, impertinent thief!" laughed Lord Shimi.

Ohn Ti, Ohn Ben's daughter, hid the five kilo bag of rice under a loose floor board, hoping her father wouldn't be caught. She was hungry, but she dared not eat now. The rice would have to supplement their meager supply of food through the coming winter.

As she dropped the partially attached floor board down, an echo seemed to come from above. Then something bounced and rolled off the flimsy roof, landing near the hut's door. She went out and saw a hand lying on the packed dirt.

She picked it up quickly, as tears burst from her eyes. The familiar hand was her father's. The tan lines left by her mother's and father's absent rings were unmistakable.

She held the hand to her face, as she collapsed onto her knees, screaming in agony. Then she inhaled sharply and turned her wet face upward.

"God, why?" she sobbed. "Please, please, end this misery!"

Her prayer was answered with the distant sound of running horses, rapidly coming closer. Ti collapsed forward onto the ground, crying loudly.

Soon, the two riders arrived, and one dismounted.

"Ohn Ti?" the standing rider spoke. "You are under arrest. You are charged with theft of communal rice rations!" Without pausing, he walked to Ti and pulled her upward. Seeing the hand she held, he snatched it from her hands and tossed it over his shoulder. He easily lifted her, still sobbing, and dumped her across the lap of the other constable.

Then, their mission almost accomplished, the constables rode away, with their horses at a walk. There was no hurry to get back to town.

The two constables walked Ohn Ti into the dark castle, one on each side of her now silent, spent form. Each one maintained a bruising grip on a frail upper arm, not caring about her pain.

They marched her along a dark hallway, with stone walls joining into a pointed arch overhead. Finally, reaching two wooden doors reinforced with iron, they faced toward the doors and waited silently.

Ohn Ti whimpered involuntarily.

One of the constables shook her arm brutally and sternly whispered, "Silence!" She could then express her pain only in the look of agony on her face and her forced breathing.

"Ohn Ti," a loud voice boomed from the top of the hallway. "After entering the courtroom, remove all clothing and jewelry and place them into the basket. Kneel in the black square, with your miserable face on the floor, and beg to be judged!"

The thundering laughter echoed through the castle as an iron bolt clanked and the two doors slowly swung open.

"Thank you, God," Ohn Ti whispered to herself, knowing that her sufferings would soon end.

Minutes later, she was standing with her arms extended and shaking, as her father had done, and she wept softly.

"SILENCE!" shouted Lord Shimi, with an echo which reverberated through the castle. "Even your pathetic father was able to face his punishment without sniveling!"

Ohn Ti's face tightened with suppressed rage and her arms were more still.

"That's better. Now, thief, how many hands should you lose? Let's see!"

The sword flashed, but there was a solid clang, a sound like the sword had struck an anvil. Ohn Ti opened her eyes and raised her face to see a man's hand, pure white, was holding the blade of the sword, just above her wrists. She looked at Lord Shimi in astonishment, but his face was a mask of rage, with confusion gradually entering his countenance. She looked back to the man's hand, with its wrist extending into nothingness, holding the sword. Everything was motionless, even her arms, and it was all too strange to understand.

"Lord Shimi!" an unfamiliar voice rumbled. It was the smooth, deep voice of an old man. But the voice carried the confidence and authority of command.

"Cease this nonsense!" The hand in front of Ti disappeared instantly and the sword with it.

With a growing light, a white form appeared to Ti's left. The glowing form coalesced into an old man in a white robe, holding a staff of pure white bamboo. The total whiteness of the man, and especially the bamboo staff, made him seem of another world, as a ghost would seem.

"On your knees, Lord Shimi!" commanded the old man.

"I kneel to no one in my own castle, old man! In fact, bow to me as you enter!"

The white old man calmly raised his staff, then struck the bottom of it forcefully against the floor. Simultaneously, Lord Shimi's knees forcefully struck the floor, and he screamed in pain and surprised rage.

Ti dropped to the floor, on all fours, and pressed her nose against the floor in terror.

"Do you not recognize your master, Lord Owa?" thundered the old man in white. "Have you forgotten that I saw you off when the transport left Earth?"

"Lord Owa! How . . . ?" asked Lord Shimi in sudden confusion.

"I landed here almost eight years ago, during an unannounced inspection tour of our colonies," said Lord Owa. "Imagine my surprise, and my disgust, when I found our colonists believed that pieces of human bodies falling from the sky was within the natural order of this planet. And was there any sign of proper management of this colony? Was there any progress toward its contracted goals? No!"

Lord Owa's "No!" echoed through the castle.

"Lord Owa," begged Lord Shimi, sounding pitifully weak in comparison.

"Silence! So, after carefully assessing the situation, I and my staff set up quarters near Moon Mountain, which we had discovered you and your minions were using as a power source for this criminal black magic."

"Lord Owa," whined Lord Shimi, even more pathetically than before. But then his mouth was wiped from his face, as if it had been nothing but face paint.

"Silence, I said!!!"

Lord Shimi felt for his missing mouth, didn't find it, and then pressed his suddenly tear-wetted face against the floor as Ti had.

"We had to spend years preparing for this confrontation, learning this planet's strange magic. But—unlike you, you black-hearted swine—we were informed by justice and our rightful sense of duty. So my powers eventually exceeded yours, and here I am!"

Lord Shimi emitted muffled cries, with his face still on the floor.

"All those years wasted, gathering my power, only to take this colony in hand! How will you repay that debt to me? How will you pay for your capricious cruelty to the colonists?"

Lord Shimi replied with only more muffled weeping.

"Oh, be gone," Lord Owa said tiredly. And Lord Shimi disappeared, as if he had never existed.

"Rise, young lady," said Lord Owa to Ti.

Ti stood, wiped tears from her face, and said, "Yes, Lord."

She saw that Lord Owa had changed into an ordinary old man in a brown robe and his bamboo staff was back to its natural green color.

"Extend your hands," said Lord Owa, quietly.

Ti extended her hands, as she had while expecting Lord Shimi's cruel punishment, trembling again. A puppy appeared in her hands, poorly balanced, and she quickly clutched it to avoid dropping it.

"That's my next-to-last act of magic, which hopefully I'll lose shortly. It's called a dog. We didn't bring them here when we established this colony, but now you and everyone else here has one. May they guard all of you from further wickedness and provide some relief from the cruel life you've led."

"Thank you, Lord," said Ti, busy restraining the squirming puppy. Very strangely to Ti, it seemed interested only in licking her face.

"My last act of magic, before I return to my home on Earth, will be to destroy Moon Mountain. Then no one else on this planet will ever again be tempted by its power." With that, Lord Owa turned and quietly walked out of Ti's life.

"Let's also go home, Dog," said Ti. "I think a better life awaits."

✦ ✦ ✦

In 2016, I was on Fort Hood, during mobilization for what would eventually be a very successful – for us, at the unit level – deployment to Afghanistan. We had accomplished most of our mobilization requirements before flying to Fort Hood, so there was some occasional down time.

At one point, I was complaining to my wife over my phone. I was bored; I had a timeline out to the year 2062 for another story in my laptop, but I'd temporarily forgotten the entire plot for that story! Worse, I didn't have any ideas for other writing projects, and it was like time in the barracks had ground to a halt.

She said, "If you want to be a science fiction writer, you should be able to write about anything."

"Like what?"

"Say, body parts falling from the sky."

"Wait, what?!?"

"But make it a happy ending this time."

"Are you kidding me?"

"And everyone gets a puppy!"

✦ ✦ ✦

THE PROTECTORS

Riding to work with his girlfriend was a very strange experience, Tom decided. Her driving didn't terrify him as much as she thought it did, but it was sometimes alarming. Her reaction time was definitely slow and she often wouldn't maintain focus on the road. Or couldn't. On the other hand, she had made a point of demonstrating her parallel parking skills on their first date. So she had some skills and perhaps more importantly, some confidence behind the wheel. *Whatever*, he thought. He knew he couldn't resist teasing her about her driving. Just not today, unless she really asked for it.

Her car was fair game too. It was a hooptie, maybe the prime example of one. She had a strong emotional attachment to it because it was her first purchase after separating from her first husband, when money was tight.

Tom maintained it now and it was certainly in better shape than when they met. But he still didn't fully trust it either.

He was riding with the passenger-side window down, enjoying the warm April breeze, and ignoring the wind noise and the rumble from the leaky old muffler. She cruised the four-lane Corridor G at about sixty miles per hour, so there wasn't much noise anyway. He thought about his new job in Charleston, which he'd taken in order to try living in West Virginia with Sheila. His military experience made it easy to get work at the phone company, but he wasn't sure their work schedules would coincide after he'd finished his training.

And there was the unwelcome baggage of a Virginian living in West Virginia.

Back to that again, he thought: Virginia versus West Virginia. He'd grown up in a podunk county in Virginia along the border with West Virginia. There'd been just as much poverty, coal smoke, ignorance, back woods, bad roads, bad football teams, noisy pick-up trucks, deer hunting, trash thrown onto the roads, deer gut piles left along the roads, pills, meth, and drunkenness as anywhere else, and certainly as many coal trains. But to every West Virginian, he'd always be different, and he'd NEVER be one of them.

He'd never think of himself as being superior. He knew himself well enough to know better. All the stupid things he'd done had drained the personal pride completely out of him, as surely as a rusty nail in a tire eventually drains out all the air. Yet it was common for West Virginians to think of themselves as inferior, which seemed crazy. From an early age, his cousins from West Virginia always resented some Virginia privilege they imagined in him. Once, they became extremely offended when he asked a second time where Sophia was. They thought that was typical Virginian disrespect; he was as deeply confused by that as he was ignorant of geography.

Only the very night before, he'd worked out a painfully relevant quotation in a cryptogram puzzle book: "Wherever an inferiority complex exists, there is a good reason for it," from Carl Jung. Those words, which had emerged a letter at a time, were dripping with pain, both observed and inflicted.

But they weren't fair, Tom decided. A reason might be preceived without it being valid. Should a man be ashamed that he works in a 28-inch high coal mine to feed his family, or should he be proud that he feeds his family? Should a boy who never had a brand-new pair of shoes, and was usually hungry all through high school be ashamed, or should he be proud of his diploma? But Tom knew it wasn't as simple as all that.

It's hard for a man who drives a filthy coal truck on filthy roads to be proud of the beauty of his home state. It's hard for kids from a town full of pillheads to be proud of where they're from, even if they steered clear of oxies and all the rest. And every time an article ranked the fifty states from best to worst on something, seeing your state consistently at the bottom of the list hit home as personally as a slap in the face.

But Tom saw the good in West Virginians which they didn't seem to notice. It might be different with the women, but if he told any of Sheila's male relatives he needed a shirt, they'd give him the one they were wearing. Not so much because the Good Book says to give, but because it would be repugnant to have a shirt on your back if a family member, or even an almost-family member, was in need.

They would be good people to have as in-laws, Tom realized.

"Want to go to the farm this weekend?" Sheila asked, interrupting his thoughts.

"Sure," he replied. "The yard will need mowing by then. And there's always fence to fix." *And it would also be great to be back home again,* he was careful NOT to think aloud. Because she'd take that to mean it would be great to be back in Virginia again. *It's the same,* he knew. *But why shouldn't he miss his home? Why should he miss it less in West Virginia than in Iraq or Afghanistan?*

And Sheila was from the famous/infamous Boone County, West Virginia.

Was there any hope for them?

She moved smoothly into the left lane to pass a tractor-trailer. He noticed "USMX 289302" on the back of the trailer, in odd block characters, at the top of the left rear door. He instantly thought of the old Ford Mustang V-8 engines, the 289 and then the 302. And wasn't the 'USMX' a prefix he'd seen on Army shipping containers, during two long deployments? As Sheila got closer to the truck, he could see that it was a trailer, not a shipping container on top of a trailer.

"What the hell?" he said aloud.

"What's wrong?"

"Weird tractor-trailer," he answered, trying to dismiss his concern. She'd often accused him of having an abnormal fascination with numbers and maybe getting wound up about a number on the back of a tractor-trailer was a little odd. Had he seen it correctly? If the trailer markings were wrong, what could he do, anyway? There was no reason to complain, so he tried to let it go.

Still, the tractor-trailer looked brand new, with an unblemished white paint job. It was unusually clean, except for bits of green and brown splatter thrown from the tires. Coming close alongside the truck, its tires looked perfectly new, except for residual muck from having been driven off road. The strong smell of cow manure, with the unmistakable stink of wild garlic the cattle had eaten with the fresh April grass, made it clear what the green splatter was.

The number 283031 was the only marking on the side door of the tractor. Odd. That was the ZIP Code where he lived in Fayetteville, North Carolina, when he was stationed at Fort Bragg, followed by the number 1. *But that didn't make it bizarre,* he thought. Wasn't there some requirement to have the name of the trucking company on the truck, or a DOT number? He wasn't sure about the Department of Transportation thing. He wasn't even sure why he was thinking about that.

"We could get the bikes out and take a ride, too." he said, trying to change the subject in his own mind. But the truck was disturbing somehow. "The weather's supposed to be nice all weekend." *Pretty,* he thought. Sheila and the West Virginia boys in his training class would be more likely to say "The weather will be pretty all weekend." He'd better not point that out to Sheila, he decided.

He then thought about getting the two DR650 on/off-road motorcycles out of the tractor shed. *They'd get cow manure on them too, unless he was very careful riding them into the yard behind his farmhouse. But how do you get cow manure on a brand-new truck? You see the damnedest things in West Virginia,* he concluded.

"Yes!" she replied. At first, he thought she was agreeing that one would see the damnedest things in West Virginia. Then he realized a West Virginia girl would never agree to that, even if she knew it to be the gospel truth.

"Can we ride to Staunton?" she asked. "I want to walk Beverly Street again."

"Sure, hon."

He thought of the restaurants there, the coffee shops, and stores with old bric-a-brac. Then he realized that she was thinking about getting them into the theater for a play. He wondered how she'd talk him into that. Not that it mattered. He'd play her little game; he liked her little games.

Sheila slowed for the traffic stopped at the intersection of Route 214. Ahead, he saw another tractor-trailer with "USMX 289302" on its left rear door. He felt a chill, despite the warm and humid air. Even if one trailer happened to be marked with the same ID number as a military shipping container, why would two trailers have the same number? He turned his head to look through the right-side mirror for the tractor-trailer behind them. It wasn't there. Had he lost track of the one she passed, and it somehow got in front of them? Had his mind wandered to Staunton that much? Finally, he did see a white tractor-trailer behind them, but he couldn't tell if it was the same one they'd passed.

"Hon, pull off to the right, at the intersection." There was a seldom-used dirt road starting from there, with an oversized paved interface from the intersection.

The road at the left was the heavily-used Route 214, to Yawkey and Alum Creek.

"What's wrong?"

The light had turned green and traffic was moving through the intersection and up the hill beyond.

"Not sure. Just pull off and get ready to get back onto Corridor G."

She signaled to the right, slowed, and turned into the paved interface area. It was sometimes used as a temporary parking area, but it was empty just then, so there was plenty of room to loop back toward Corridor G.

He scanned the traffic that had been behind them as the vehicles zoomed by. In less than a minute, the trailing "USMX 289302" tractor-trailer passed them.

"Get back on the road when you can."

She had to wait only a few seconds, then accelerated out onto Corridor G.

"Pass those two white tractor-trailers ahead of you."

"What's going on?"

"I need to check something. Just drive, and watch the road."

She wasn't going fast enough.

"Go at least sixty-five. That's the speed limit here, so don't worry about that."

"I know," she said, in a tone from somewhere between you're-criticizing-my-driving and you're-dissing-

West-Virginia-again. But he was too focused on the trucks to be annoyed.

They were soon passing the first 'USMX 289302' tractor-trailer again.

"The license plate on the trailer is 'Apportioned 283031,'" he said. An alarm went off in his head. "That can't be right! That's the same number as on the truck door!" And there was no state indicated, either.

"What number? What's with you and numbers all the time?"

His mind raced. He looked for another license plate on the back of the tractor as they went by it. He didn't see one. *Wasn't that wrong too?*

"Hold on," he said, as he looked over the side of the tractor more closely this time. "283031" was on the door and the window was darkly tinted. The truck didn't seem to be making the typical diesel-engine noises, or any engine noise at all, just the whirr of the tires on the concrete. Weird! He wondered if the driver was watching him through that dark side window and thinking he was too nosy. So Tom turned his head to the front, so as to not to look overly conspicuous. He moved only his eyes to search for the license plate on the front of the truck, using the right-side mirror.

When it came into view, it looked a little like 283031, but being backwards in the mirror, he wasn't sure. He decided not to hang out the window for a look back.

"What's 'apportioned' mean?" Sheila asked.

He turned around in the car, to look out the back window at the license plate. But it was too late to see it clearly by then.

"I have no idea." He turned back around.

"What's going on?" she said, really starting to be concerned.

"Please pass that other truck."

"I don't know why you won't—"

"Hon, I'm really trying to figure this out right now. Just watch the road, pretty please."

He could see the other "USMX 289302" tractor-trailer ahead. Soon, they were close enough to see the license plate on the back.

"Apportioned 283031!" he read. "Holy shit!"

"Isn't that the same as the other truck?"

"Yes. That can't be right!"

There was mud and cow manure splatter on the second truck, maybe more than on the other one. The second truck's door was also marked with the same 283031 number and it was just as brand-new. It had new tires, clean except for the fresh muck. And except for tire noise, the truck wasn't producing any sound.

Tom struggled to make sense of it all. *The trucks had to be some kind of fakes,* he thought. *Some kind of inexact copies of real trucks, but exact copies of each other. But what's the point in cloning fake trucks? Who in the world would do that? And why had they apparently been driven, brand spanking new, out from a cow pasture?*

He thought about calling this in to the state police. *But how would they respond to all this? Would they respond at all? Or would they just detain him for an urgently-needed psych evaluation?*

They were approaching the intersection for Childress Road and Eagle Drive, just ahead and to the left of the second truck. The light had turned red and traffic was slowing quickly.

He didn't fully understand what was happening, but felt there was no other choice but to take action. He could pay Sheila cash for her P.O.S. car anyway.

So he yelled, "Stop behind that car!" as he reached over and yanked the wheel to the right.

Sheila screamed, "TOM!" and braked harder as they swerved into the right lane, close behind the car ahead of the lead truck. Glancing at the right-side mirror again, he saw the truck swerve onto the shoulder, slowing rapidly. He yanked the wheel to the right again. There was a deep screeching of large tires sliding and the truck bumped into the back of the car.

"Oh my God!" Sheila yelled. "You wrecked my car!"

They were stopped on the shoulder. The truck was stopped close behind them.

He got out of the car and approached the truck. It was silent. He raised his hands, shrugging an "I'm sorry/I-don't-know" gesture. The license plate on the front of the truck had the same Apportioned 283031 number as the plates on the trailers. The truck's driver remained motionless, staring straight ahead. Tom dropped his arms and continued to the driver's side door. He knocked on the door, but didn't really expect it to open. It remained closed. He couldn't see through the driver's side window, so he climbed up onto the side steps of the truck. Still not being able to see through the window, he cupped his hands to his face as he peered in more closely. The driver appeared to be some kind of plastic mannequin. Its face was as blank as a freshly-molded doll's head, before eyes were painted onto it. It remained motionless.

He jumped down and turned to Sheila's car. She was standing beside it with her door open, looking at Tom like he'd gone crazy. The light had changed and traffic was accelerating through the intersection, apparently oblivious to what had just happened.

"Get in the other side of the car. I'm driving."

"But we can't leave—"

"We can't stay, either. Move!"

She turned and ran around the front of the car with her hands up near her shoulders, using a delightfully jiggly motion he couldn't help but notice. But there was no time for that nonsense. He got in, slammed the driver's-side door, and started the car. She hurried to pull her door closed after the engine had started.

He looked back using the left-side mirror and saw the road was clear. The first fake truck had pulled onto the shoulder, behind the other one.

He gunned the car across to the left turn lane.

"Tom!"

The left turn light was red, but seeing a long break in traffic coming the other way, he U-turned sharply and gunned it again.

"Let's hope those things are programmed to ignore small traffic incidents and go on about their business!"

"What are you talking about? What business? How badly is my car damaged and where are we going?"

"I don't know what's going on. But there was no driver in that truck and it wasn't even a real truck. The car is fine, good enough to get the hell out of here anyway. I think we need to go to the farm. Is there anything in Madison you need?"

"All my stuff is there. I live there!"

"I mean do you have enough stuff at the farm to stay there a while? Clothes and such?"

"Yes. But what about work? What about the cats?"

"Work will have to wait. And Mary can come over and look after the cats while we're at the farm. She's done it before." He glanced at the gas gauge. It showed the tank only about a quarter full. *Not enough*, he thought. He drove south on Corridor G at about seventy-five miles per hour.

When Tom turned off Corridor G in Danville, Sheila was even more unhappy.

"Route 85 goes right through Madison," Sheila fumed. "I need to stop at my house!"

"Hon, I have a bad feeling about this." He wasn't sure what else to say. But it might be good to drive his pickup to the farm and leave her car. And his pickup's gas tank was almost full. "How much time do you need?"

"Five minutes."

"Okay. Let's do it. We'll take the truck from there. Five minutes!"

Five minutes after parking in front of her house, Tom was sitting in his pickup, alone. Following a hunch, he got out of the truck and looked for tools behind the driver's seat. Only an old, large pair of fence pliers was there. No screwdrivers or wrenches. He grabbed the pliers, walked to Sheila's car, and ripped the license plate off the rear bumper, tearing the aluminum away from the mounting screws. Being registered in West Virginia, it had no front license plate. He put the pliers and the torn license plate behind the pickup's seat.

At the eight-minute mark, Tom had called into his work while sitting in the truck, still alone. As usual, his call went to his boss's voicemail. The breathy, female automated voice announced that the mailbox was full. He then began a text message to his boss's work cell phone.

Suddenly, twin thunderclaps echoed across the bright blue sky.

This is really not good, he thought, as if some dark premonition had been fulfilled. Dropping his phone, blew the pickup's horn and got out of the truck. He searched around for the source of the noises and saw nothing. Then he realized that the hills must be blocking the view to the source.

Sheila came out within a minute, pulling a large wheeled bag.

"Don't honk your horn at me!" she said, walking up to the front of the pickup.

Tom took the bag and lifted it into the back of the pickup. It was heavy, but he didn't feel like asking what was in it.

"The power just went off," Shelia said.

"It doesn't matter. Let's get out of here."

Sirens started sounding in the distance.

"What about the food in the freezer?"

"Forget it. We need to get out of here!"

"What about the cats?"

"Hon, we've got to go!"

The drive south on Route 85 was uneventful, but faster than it usually was, even though traffic was heavier than usual. Soon they started up Bolt Mountain and turned onto Route 99. Tom knew where he wanted to stop next: one of the pull-off areas, with the wide views from the many high points along the road. Soon, they reached one.

"Let's stop here and have a look."

There was a gigantic plume of smoke and dust to the north-northwest, with its flattened upper part trailing to the east.

"Is that Charleston?" Sheila asked.

"WAS Charleston."

"Oh, my God!" Her eyes locked onto the enormous dust cloud and she held back a sob with both hands over her mouth.

He scanned to the east, as much as he could see around the trees. "It looks like Beckley wasn't hit." More to the southeast, there was a smudge of smoke in the distance, partly concealed by the trees. "Maybe Roanoke was."

"Those trucks were hauling bombs, weren't they?"

"I guess so, hon. They might have been remote-controlled nuclear weapons. Or maybe those things were automated enough to drive themselves to their targets."

"They could have gone off when you wrecked my car!"

"Maybe. But they weren't at their targets yet. I guess we didn't pose enough of a threat for them to self-destruct."

"Could we have stopped them?"

"How? We had no weapons. There was nobody to shoot anyway. I don't think those vehicles even had normal diesel engines. So what could we do?"

"Where do you think they came from?"

Tom paused, as a thought coalesced in his mind.

"Hon, I think those trucks were dropped, freshly copied, into some out-of-the way cow pasture last night. There was no road dirt on them, only mud and cow manure."

"Who drops brand-new tractor-trailers into cow pastures?"

"I thought about that. I decided no one in this world would do such a thing."

"Then aliens did this?"

"That's the only sense I can make of it. And for some reason I can't imagine, they didn't want to drop their weapons onto the cities directly." He didn't want to speculate any further with her. There was no point in it and thinking about it was too distracting now. *But would they nuke the cities, using the kind of weapons we'd use ourselves, maybe while making a false record claiming we'd done it to ourselves? If so, a false record for whom? But whatever was going on, it didn't seem to be over yet.*

Tom looked to the southeast, thinking about the drive into Virginia. "The dust and smoke over Roanoke seems bigger, like—"

Bright light flashed across the sky. Both turned to see a fiery cloud rising from the northwest, obviously closer than Charleston. The fiery light within the cloud faded as a mushroom of smoke formed at its top. A thin, slanted, smoky streak was visible, from the base of the cloud to the top of the sky.

"Oh my God," Sheila said. "That's Madison!"

Tom knew it had to be, but was quite confused. "Why nuke Madison?" he wondered aloud. He looked back to the east, and saw the much larger Beckley area untouched. He looked all around, searching the horizon for other explosions. There were no other new ones. "Why no others?"

"Oh my God—," Sheila repeated, her eyes filling with tears.

"They tried to kill us," Tom realized aloud.

"What?" Sheila said, turning to him. "But we're here!"

"Say there was a video feed from those trucks, whether it was used to control them or not. Then it must have picked up your license plate, and then us going back toward Madison. Maybe they looked up your address from it." He struggled to put it all together, realizing their lives were probably at stake. "They would need to access the DMV records or have a copy from before Charleston got blown up. That means they would have to know how to read the data. If all that's true, they looked up your address from your license plate, got your address, and there goes Madison. They must not have surveillance on us, not in real time anyway. Otherwise that bomb would have gone off right here."

A noise like a distant rifle shot, then a sharp thunderclap swept over them, followed by a chorus of echoes. Tom wished he'd timed the difference between the flash and the sound. But the new explosion had to be over Madison.

"Why are they trying to kill us?"

"It has to be because we know about the trucks. It must be. No one was supposed to know it wasn't some other country attacking us, or domestic terrorism, or whatever. They're covering up that it's an alien attack."

"Are you sure?"

"No! I don't know. What else could it be? They haven't blown up larger cities, like Beckley. It doesn't look like Huntington was hit either. If they aren't after us, why blow up a small town like Madison?"

Tom watched the plume rise from Madison, then noticed the one from Charleston had moved closer.

"I think that dust is coming this way. Let's get going."

Sheila was looking toward Madison with cheeks wet with tears. Tom turned and embraced her.

"First, the people I work with," she sobbed. "Now my friends and family are dead! And the cats!"

He pulled her closer and they stood together for a moment.

"It could have been us too," Tom said. "Could still be us. We gotta go."

Route 3 into Beckley was congested near every gas station, but they made their way through. Police were trying to keep the road clear as much as possible.

"There's no cell service," Sheila said. "And I don't see any sign the power's on."

"There's no point in waiting in line for gasoline, then."

He turned on the radio, but there were no stations transmitting, either AM or FM. Gradually, they made their way to I-64 and started east. State police cars were parked at some of the exits.

"Crap. I hope they aren't thinking about closing the interstate!" Tom said, wishing right away he hadn't.

"Should we tell them about the trucks?"

"I don't think so, hon. I think those trucks are all blown into dust and radioactive fallout anyway."

He didn't want to talk to the state police. The more he thought about it, the more he dreaded having them file that kind of report. Who would eventually see it?

"We should get the word out. We might be the only ones who know about those trucks," Sheila said.

"That's what I'm concerned about. Let's assume they have access to state records, even now. So if they are after us, then we don't want a police report filed."

"I get it. If we did, they'd know we got away from Madison and they'd pick up a fresh trail on us!"

"Smart girl. We'll get the word out, but let's figure out how to do that without giving ourselves away."

"Smart boy!"

Tom just grinned at her, looked back to the road, and hoped—like so many times before—that things would be better back home.

Just after getting to Covington, they used exit 14 to get off I-64.

"Let's see if the Walmart's open," Tom said, turning south onto Durant Road.

Within a minute, they could see that the road to the Walmart was blocked with a barricade and a police car. And the Walmart building was burning.

"I'd say not," Sheila said.

"Looks like we missed the excitement."

"What do you think happened?"

"What always happens when people panic, I guess."

"How much stuff is there in the farmhouse?"

"I'm not sure," Tom said. "I mean, how much is enough? How much will we need?"

Sheila only turned her head away. Tom knew he hadn't said the right thing.

The farmhouse seemed normal when they arrived. But there was no electricity and that meant no running water from the well.

Tom said, "Leave the refrigerator and freezer closed. Look around everywhere else and see how much water there is."

"Are you getting hungry?"

"Yes, but let's gather up the water we have first. In the hall closet there's a gallon jug of water, or part of one, I was using for the iron. Start gathering the camping gear too. We're going to need it. I left some distilled water out in the shed for engine coolant. I'll go get that."

"Did you set mousetraps?"

"Yes, in the basement. I'll empty them when I get back in."

Tom found two unopened gallons of distilled water in the shed. He checked his two five-gallon plastic gasoline cans. One was empty and the other was about half full. The one-gallon can with two-stroke mix for his chainsaw was about half full also. *Not good,* he thought. But there was enough two-stroke oil for several more gallons of two-stroke mix. He'd have to check how much gasoline was in the truck and the motorcycles later. He took the water back inside.

Sheila had cleared off the kitchen table and placed a water jug on it. It was about half full. His propane gas camp stove was there too, with two propane cylinders, a plastic container of wooden matches, and the little coffee percolator they used while camping. One of the propane cylinders had a white plastic cap and looked new. He picked them up and found the one without the cap to be slightly lighter. According to their labels, they contained 16.4 ounces of fuel when full. An ominous feeling rose in him. He set the full cylinder aside and screwed the single-burner stove onto the top of the used one.

Tom heard the toilet flush and knew that the tank wouldn't refill. That was three or four gallons of drinkable water gone, but he decided that he wouldn't raise the issue with Sheila.

She came into the kitchen and said, "Sorry, I flushed the toilet before I thought about it."

"It's okay. I decided I wouldn't want to drink out of the toilet tank anyway," he lied diplomatically. "Want some dinner?"

"Yes!"

Because he usually cooked in his house, he opened the refrigerator and checked its contents. There were three packages of shredded cheese, a new block of sharp cheddar, an unopened but slightly expired package of flour tortillas, eight unexpired eggs, and several condiments.

He kept out four eggs, some shredded cheddar, and the flour tortillas. "Fried eggs and quesadillas for dinner?" he asked.

The rest he placed in the freezer, where they'd stay cold a little longer. There wasn't much else in the freezer: some large freezer bags full of last fall's venison, some freezer-burned chicken legs and thighs, some microwave-in-the-bag vegetables, and a loaf of bread. He moved the bread to the refrigerator to thaw and to cool the other contents a little.

"Sure. What are we drinking?"

"There's some beer in the refrigerator and a bottle of white wine."

"Let's have the wine. We should celebrate being alive."

"Good idea, hon," Tom said. A very good idea. He took a clean frying pan out of the dishwasher, set it on the table, and lit the camp stove.

"Let's start with the wine," Sheila said.

"That's my girl!"

✦ ✦ ✦

The sun was low in the western sky during dinner and its light streamed onto the kitchen table. Tom's pump shotgun was now leaning against one of the chairs. He'd taken it out of the safe and loaded it.

"Let's work out what we know from today," Tom said. "Knowledge is power."

"Do we know anything before the trucks?" Sheila asked.

"No, not that I can think of."

"Then let's start with them. What was the first thing you noticed?"

"The numbers on the two trailers, USMX 289302, on both." He tried to recall first seeing them. "The letters were blocky and weird. Now that I think about it, they weren't in the kind of font someone would use on their equipment. Companies are careful about the markings and graphics on their trucks. But that's not what caught my attention. Numbers like that are for shipping containers, not trailers. And even if someone put numbers like that on trailers, they shouldn't be duplicated."

"And all of their license plate numbers were the same?"

"Yes, the same number was on all the trailer and truck license plates, and also on the doors of the trucks." He thought for a minute. "What does all that tell us about the aliens?"

"I don't know. What?"

"Well, doesn't it seem sloppy, not having more accurate reproductions of the trucks or their markings? They were turning out exact copies, one truck to the next, not bothering with details much. It seems lazy, as if making each truck unique wasn't worth the trouble."

"They were about to get blown up, if they had bombs in them. So details wouldn't matter."

"Yes, but it still tells us something about the aliens, doesn't it? Why make Earth trucks, but poor copies of Earth trucks? The license plates didn't have any markings for which state they were from, either."

"Was that because identical trucks were used in attacks all over the country?"

"I hadn't thought of that," Tom said. "Let's say that's true. But that means they didn't understand that tractor-trailers go all over the country and license plates of a given state wouldn't look out of place in any other state."

"So they don't do details."

"I think the attack itself was very detailed and very effective. But they didn't study our equipment carefully, or they're sloppy with details that, well, I'm not sure—"

"Maybe what we see doesn't matter," Sheila said. "We're not that important to them."

"That rings true. But maybe they've underestimated us and their sloppiness will be an advantage we can use."

✦ ✦ ✦

That evening, Sheila embraced Tom when he emerged from the bathroom.

"I love you," she whispered. "And I'm glad we're surviving. Just don't say anything about 'repopulating the world.'"

"You know how many—"

"Don't."

"But how many more times—"

"You want a cliché? Here ya go: 'Shut up and kiss me!'"

Later, Sheila was cuddled tightly against Tom's back. "What should we do tomorrow?" she purred.

"Repopulate the world."

She laughed, then said, "Seriously."

"Water is the big thing. I want to pull one of the concrete covers part-way off the old hand-dug well and see if it's still usable. We used water from it while I grew up here, before my dad had the deep well dug. The old shallow-well pump is still in the basement, but I doubt it's any good now, even if we had electricity."

"Then how will you get water out of the well?"

"We'll have to use a bucket and a rope."

"Will it be safe to drink?"

"Probably. We didn't treat it in all those years. I remember it was rust-colored at times, but minerals won't hurt us. Maybe we should treat it, just to be safe."

"Boil it?"

"We can boil some, but we don't have enough fuel to boil all the water we need to drink. There's some bleach in the basement, over the washing machine. They say you can treat water with it. But I'm not sure how much to use."

Sheila rolled away, then said, "Warm me up."

Tom spooned up against her tightly, as she scooted toward him. "Love ya, hon."

"Love you more."

The next morning, Tom looked through the refrigerator and planned breakfast. He made coffee in the little percolator, then took a cup to Sheila, who was still in bed.

"Coffee's up," he said. "Even if you're not."

"I'm cold!" she whined.

He decided not to apply the body-heat solution. "We've got stuff to do, old slug-a-bed!"

He went to the basement with a shopping bag because he'd forgotten to empty the mousetraps the night before. Normally, he'd scoop up the dead mice and the traps together, dump them into the bag, tie it closed, and take it out to the trash can with whatever trash was in the kitchen. But today, he emptied just the dead mice into the shopping bag and dropped the nasty traps back onto the floor. *We might need to re-use those now*, he thought.

Next, he started a fire in the old wood stove with some of the wood left over from the winter. The stove would pull the dank, cold air from the basement, which smelled a little of dead mice, and heat the kitchen above.

He took the shopping bag up to the kitchen, dropped it into the trash can, tied its bag closed, and took the trash out. It was cold for April, and cloudy. He wasn't sure if the clouds were normal rain clouds or fallout. *Probably some of both,* he thought.

Going back to the basement, he found the kindling to be burning well, so he put some larger pieces of wood into the stove.

He returned to the kitchen, put some brown rice on to boil, sat at the table, drank his coffee, and thought about their situation. When the rice was done, he drained it, put it back on the camp stove, and added a can of pinto beans. He added a little water and some chili powder, crushed red pepper, and some ground cumin. After it returned to a boil, he divided it between two bowls and served it up covered with shredded cheddar.

"Breakfast is ready!" he called toward the bedroom.

Sheila emerged with her coffee and bed-head hair, wearing a thick bathrobe and slippers. Keeping her coffee cup well clear, she leaned into Tom and gave him some pats on his back which felt like, "GOOD BOY for providing coffee and food!"

"The stuff in the freezer isn't thawed yet," he said. "Maybe we can have chicken tonight. I didn't want eggs again, so it's beans and rice."

"Good," she said, already starting to eat.

"The coffee has the last of the water we should drink from the jugs. After breakfast, how 'bout finding water containers, and cleaning them out with some of the water we have?"

"Sure. I think there are some old kitty litter buckets here."

"With their lids?"

"I think so. I don't throw them away."

"Good. Those would be great for purifying water. I'll keep a bucket of unpurified water in the bathroom, too. We can pour it into the toilet for flushing."

"I'll wash the dishes after you get water."

"Okay. I'll keep a kitty-litter bucket of treated water on the counter, next to the sink."

"I'd rather have one of those blue water containers we use for camping," Sheila said. They have spigots."

"Good idea."

After breakfast, Tom got his .40 auto out of the gun safe, still in its nylon holster. He loaded it, threaded his belt through the holster, and went out to the old well.

It was very close to the road, so Tom knew that it could become a popular attraction, and he wasn't comfortable with that. The massive old concrete base and the two-piece concrete covers were covered with last year's vines and leaves. So he went to the shed for a hatchet and a broom.

Back at the well, he began to clear it off. Within minutes, he heard a car coming. Only then did he realize how little traffic there had been on the road, so he stopped working to watch the car. It soon stopped near the well, and the driver rolled down his side window. Tom saw that it was Mark Weston, a neighbor.

"Hi, Tom," Mark said.

"Hi, Mark."

"I wanted to ask about that well. You have some time?"

"Sure."

"Let me park. I'll be right back."

Mark drove to the driveway, parked next to Tom's truck, and walked to the well.

"I figured this thing would draw attention," Tom said.

"I remembered it was here. I wouldn't bother you, but we're out of water."

"Let's see if there's anything in it."

Tom swept the debris off the covers, then he and Mark lifted one slightly, using the rusty, looped rebar handles protruding from its top.

"It's heavier than it looks," Mark said.

"Set it on this corner." They rotated the cover counterclockwise and balanced it on one corner of the square base.

Through the gap, they could see dark water about thirty feet down. Some tree roots were hanging from the rock-lined sides of the well, but it looked fine otherwise. As Tom remembered from years ago, the water was moving toward the southwest, as indicated by the waving drift of the slight ripples.

"Good," Tom said. "I've seen it a lot lower than that, but I don't think it's ever been empty. I guess as long as there's water anywhere in this valley, there'll be water in this well. And I don't think people dipping out of it will affect its level much, if at all. So you're welcome to take what you want."

"I sure appreciate it."

"But I have to say, other people will see there's water here, and I don't like the idea of a crowd forming this close to the house."

"And getting crazy, like people do," Mark said.

"Exactly."

"I don't want you put out over providing water. So if you don't mind, I'll let the neighbors know they can get some water here and organize some guards. I have some buckets and some rope. I'll set those up and they'll be watched, too."

"I can't have people milling around the house. And we should keep the road clear."

"We could have them park and line up in that hayfield across the road and allow only two at a time to cross the road and use the well. I'll talk to Andrews about using that field, but he's sure not doing anything with it."

"Good. Thanks."

"Thank you, Tom. There must be a lot of people without water. Until the power's back on, anyway."

"You're welcome. But the thanks should go to whoever dug that thing. I still can't imagine how they did it, with water running down there."

"Hard to say. I've always heard this valley's just like Swiss cheese. Water runs out of the ground at the start of Blue Spring Run. It must be the same water."

"Can people get water there?"

"I guess so, but it would be a long climb back up to the road. And it's really steep and rocky in that draw."

"May as well be on the moon, then."

"Yep."

They watched the water flowing in the well. Tom remembered something he had to do.

"Mark, I need to tell you a story. A true story."

He told Mark about the trucks near Charleston and the destruction of Madison.

"Wow, that's a hell of a thing!" Mark said.

"They don't want that story to get out. So get it out, if you don't mind."

"Sure. We only heard about Roanoke gone, but no details. But this! Yeah, I think the word will spread pretty fast."

The slow movement of the dark well water seemed like a living window into an underground world, but it remained opaque. For an instant, Tom wondered why it didn't reflect anything above, but there was nothing.

"Tommy, I should get to work," Mark finally said.

"Yeah, me too."

"I'll be back in a while. Thanks again!"

Mark soon drove back toward his house, leaving Tom to wonder if he was doing the right thing. He was still uneasy about people hanging around. And anyone nearby could get killed during another attempt to silence him and Sheila. The sky was darkening. He left the cover as it was, put his tools away, and went back into the house.

Sheila had kitty litter buckets clean, covered again, and stacked in the kitchen. She'd also brought the bleach up from the basement.

"Thanks for building a fire," she said.

"Sure, hon."

"Who was that out there?"

"Mark Weston. He's going to organize people getting water from the well. There's still flowing water in it, so people should be able to dip out of it without affecting the water level. It probably runs underground to Blue Spring Run anyway. I'm just worried it'll end up being a three-ring circus out there."

"Want to get some water now?"

"No. I didn't see any rope in the shed, and Mark said he'd bring some. If I know him, he'll have something set up soon. So let's wait a while."

"Okay. There's no hurry."

"I told him what happened yesterday. The word should spread quickly."

"Did he know anything else about what's happened?"

"Nothing much. So if a sneak attack on us was part of the plan, that part worked."

That afternoon, Tom looked out the window and saw activity at the water point. There was already a line of people in Andrews' field. He walked out to see what was happening.

Mark and one of the other Westons were sitting on lawn chairs near the well, with shotguns across their laps. Mark got up, but the other went back to watching people dip from the well.

"Hello again, Tommy. Come see what we did."

"Sure. How's it going?"

"Smooth as glass. Look at the rope we set up."

Tom saw that they'd sunk a wooden post near the well, and tied the upper end of the rope to it. "Good idea," he thought aloud.

"That will keep someone from dropping the rope and bucket into the well," Mark said. "Check the sign." They walked around two people Tom didn't recognize and up onto the road.

A sign, hand-lettered in black over plywood painted white, was attached to another new post. It read:

--- FREE WATER ---

- No weapons allowed!
- Every day, 8 AM to 6 PM only!
- Line up across the road, in the field.
- Keep the road clear. No standing on the road!
- Only two at a time at the well.
- Take as much as you can carry back to the field.
- Wait in line again to cross road again.
- Landowner is permitted to get water when he wants, without waiting in line.
- If you take water, a responsible adult in your family should volunteer for guard duty. See Mark Weston at his house, 6:30 PM daily.
- Follow directions from landowner and guards. Breaking these rules means loss of water privileges!

Tom was impressed and said so.

"Anna is making another sign, for where people are driving into the field. It'll say 'No Weapons at Well.' That should keep people from walking over here armed before they see this sign."

"This is really good, Mark. I couldn't have done any better."

"Thanks for the water, Mister," said a teenager at the well, filling his own kitty-litter buckets.

"You're welcome," said Tom.

"We've had some volunteers for guards already," Mark said. "I'll ask about the people I don't know, then I'll have someone sit with them until they're known to be reliable. But it seems people are serious about keeping this well safe. Maybe we'll end up having enough guards so we can work only two-hour shifts."

"Mark, thanks for organizing this. It's a big weight off my shoulders. I'm going to get some buckets."

"No problem, Tommy." And Mark went back to watching the people at the well.

As Tom walked to the house, he marveled at how much life can change, and how quickly.

Two days later, Tom was fetching water shortly before noon, during a drizzly break between rain showers. He wondered if contamination was falling with the drizzle and wished he'd brought out the covers for the kitty litter buckets. It would be great to know the level of contamination, he thought, but realized that Geiger counters hadn't been manufactured or sold for years, maybe decades.

He didn't know the two teenagers on guard, but they seemed respectful and attentive. As he filled the second bucket, his thoughts turned to bleach. He'd decided to reduce the bleach to a half teaspoon per bucket. He thought that would be safe, and he hoped the water would taste better. Already, he was sick of the taste of bleach.

A chirping noise was suddenly heard. The guards stood up, holding their shotguns at a low-ready position. Soon, the chirping noise increased as a brown delivery truck approached Tom's driveway. The chirping was loud enough to function as a siren. At the mailbox, the truck stopped. A mechanical arm opened his mailbox, put a white sheet of something into it, and closed it; all in one deft motion.

As the truck started toward them, Tom stopped work and placed his hands over his ears. When the truck passed, he could see that the original door had been removed from the right side, and some kind of gun had been attached by welding a gun mount onto the door frame. The gun was folded downward, but it seemed ready for immediate use. There appeared to be another gun on the other side of the truck. Between the guns was a robot, crudely humanoid in shape, with an equally crude, dull-metal surface. It didn't seem interested in the people at the well.

"A robot!" one of the teenage guards said.

"It looked like it was stamped out of sheet metal," said the other.

"Mass produced, cheaply as possible, I'd guess," said Tom. "So there are probably a lot more like it."

As the truck sped off, the chirping siren faded. Tom left his buckets at the well and went to his mailbox. In it was a wad of thin, white plastic. Taking it out, he unfolded it and read:

People of Earth

In accordance with the provisions of the Galactic Charter, the Central Committee of Zone 53 has declared a state of emergency on your planet. This action became necessary to end unlawful warfare causing excessive loss of life and environmental damage.

You have been liberated from the oppressive governmental, police, and corporate entities which caused that unlawful warfare. From this day onward, all inhabitants on your planet are private citizens, and free.

Within the specifications of the Galactic Charter, you will be provided with the necessary nutrients, medicines, and fuel to maintain life. Because water is abundant on your planet, the responsibility of obtaining it is yours.

At [1148 AM] the next day, the same vehicle will return to deliver food, fuel, and further documentation. From that day onward, the residents at this address must present themselves near this mailbox, away from the roadway, to be counted. The rations placed into the mailbox will be calculated based on the number of residents observed, on a daily basis.

If the delivery vehicle is delayed or molested in any way, rations for this route will be suspended for three days. During the suspension, residents must present themselves near the mailbox as usual. On the day the suspension is lifted, the rations will be delivered based on an average count of residents for that day, and for every day of the suspension. If the delivery vehicle is delayed or molested again, the suspension of rations will be doubled, and doubled again for each subsequent incident.

Weapons of all kinds are prohibited. Any display of weapons, from the next day onward, constitutes an unlawful breach of the peace imposed by the state of emergency. Any weapons made visible to operators of delivery vehicles shall constitute an offense punishable as described above.

Future documents will describe employment opportunities within this area when they become available. Employment in positions approved under the state of emergency will be rewarded only with larger rations. No monetary systems will be used and are hereby prohibited from this day onward, as those systems resulted in oppression of workers and created the prerequisites for unlawful war.

"Oh, shit," Tom said. Feeling dazed, he shuffled to the well to get his buckets. As he walked, he carelessly refolded the slightly wet plastic and stuffed it into his pants pocket.
"What's that?" one of the young guards asked.
"Bad news. Don't have any weapons out here from now on." He carried his buckets into the house.
"What was going on out there?" Sheila asked.
"We're in trouble. The aliens know exactly how to enslave humans."

Still following their usual custom, Tom cooked dinner: venison chili stew with brown rice and a can of corn, topped with the last of the shredded cheddar.

"We'll need to eat all of this, with no way to save it," he said. "Dig in."

Sheila was apparently still thinking about the inventory they'd performed earlier. "How long do you think our food will last?"

"Well, we'll need to use everything in the freezer first. So lots of protein for a while. Then with all of the random canned stuff, the rice, cornmeal, sardines, crackers, pickles, and such, maybe there's enough for two weeks. Maybe three."

"I hate sardines."

"Sorry, but it's what we have. I sure bought a lot of them, and cornmeal. I'm not sure why. I wish we had more brown rice." Changing to a more positive thought, he said, "I can make cornmeal mush. Boiled, then fried. We have a second bottle of cooking oil."

"Plenty of salt, too. More than two pounds."

"That's very good. We can use it to preserve venison, if I see a deer."

"What about getting food from the aliens? Do you think it's safe to let them see us?"

Tom ate his chili awhile and thought about it. "I think we're in the clear. If they had found a link back to me, or to the farm, we'd be toast already."

"I was thinking about that too. Your truck is still registered in Virginia, and you applied for your job from here, right? So there shouldn't be public records tying you to Madison."

"I hope not."

After dinner, Tom brewed some hot tea.

Serving it, he said, "I'm concerned about the food we can find here. We don't seem to have any seed to start a garden and deer will soon be scarce, with everyone around here after them. I read once that deer were wiped out in this area during the 1930s. And there will be even more people hunting now."

"I wish I'd brought my seeds from Madison. I had plenty for a garden."

"There was no time for that. Maybe we can find some, or trade for some. We'll have to talk to the neighbors. Until then, I think we should stand out front, be counted, and start taking rations from the aliens."

"I think so too."

"The alternative would be to hold back for a few days, to see what happens. But that might raise suspicions and I don't want them paying any special attention to us. And I'm curious what they'll bring on the first day."

"Where would they get food for us? I can't imagine aliens shipping food here for everyone."

"It's hard to say. After seeing how soon they began modifying and using those brown delivery trucks, maybe they'll distribute captured food supplies as well."

"I'd rather eat food from Earth, if I had the choice!"

"It's not just the food. They said there would be fuel, too. These two propane cylinders won't last long. We don't have much gasoline or firewood either, to put it bluntly. So getting our fuel ration will be important."

"You know how cold it gets in this valley. We'll have to have the firewood."

"Yes," Tom agreed. "Without knowing what fuel ration they're planning, I don't know what to think. But I can't imagine them handing out firewood. Not in this area, anyway. Trees are more plentiful than water, and we know what they think about that. Let's conserve all the gasoline we have for getting firewood."

"Okay. There doesn't seem to be anywhere else to go, anyway. I want to start a garden, one way or another. There are seeds somewhere around here. I'll find some."

"Good."

"We left pumpkins out by the front steps last Halloween, and some split open. So we might already have wild pumpkin plants starting by the front porch."

"Good, sweets. I'll get after Bambi and try drying some venison."

The next morning, Tom was cleaning his .30-30 rifle. His thoughts ranged from deer hunting, to wishing he had more ammunition, to how useless the rifle would be against the aliens and their equipment. Then he refocused on deer hunting, trying to remain positive.

Yet the process of cleaning a weapon, which during his Army days had usually calmed his mind and provided reassurance through readiness and preparedness, offered no solace. Instead, each drop of oil and every bore patch he used only reminded him of how short his supplies were. But worse than running out of ammunition, gun cleaning supplies, bleach, food, or anything else, was running out of time. And he felt he was.

"11:30," Sheila said.

"Okay." Tom put away the .30-30 and the cleaning materials.

"I have your rain jacket," Sheila said, holding it for him.

"Thanks, hon."

He took the jacket and finished getting dressed. Early that morning, they'd decided on ball caps with brims pulled low and rain jackets with hoods up. The possibility of being recognized from the tractor-trailer incident seemed unlikely, but the weather made it easy to partly cover their faces and limit their level of visibility.

"Ready?" Tom asked.

"Yes. I want to get a look at that thing."

They went outside and walked to the driveway.

"It's good that it's raining," Tom said. "I'm not sure, but it seems if there's been fallout from the bombs, it's getting washed off the house and into the ground." He held out his hand to catch some rain and watched for any accumulation of dirt on his palm. There didn't seem to be any. "If there is any fallout dust, at least it's not blowing around dry. We wouldn't want to inhale it."

"Do you think it's getting into the water?"

"I don't think so. Any fallout should be caught in the soil and filtered out of the groundwater," he said. But he wasn't sure about what would be falling directly into the well. "The well is always open now, so there might be some possibility of contamination. But I'm hoping whatever doesn't sink to the bottom gets washed away in the moving current."

He looked toward the well and wasn't surprised to see it deserted. The others would be waiting at their mailboxes, or hiding. Hiding suddenly sounded like a good idea.

The chirping siren could be heard again.

"Is that the robot truck?" Sheila asked.

"That's him."

The same brown delivery truck rolled up to the mailbox, braking heavily. They could see the robot, with its large bulbous head, still behind a short-barreled gun and its mount. It didn't seem to observe them in any noticeable way. As quickly as the day before, the robot produced a white package from somewhere behind it, placed it into the mailbox, and sped away.

Tom realized he hadn't bothered to cover his ears and heard a faint ringing as the chirping faded.

"I'm wearing earplugs out here tomorrow," he said.

"Let's see what we got," Sheila said, walking to the mailbox. She returned with a bulky white plastic envelope, about the size of a small shoebox. She was trying to tear it open by hand, but couldn't.

"Let's take it in. It looks like we'll need something to cut that open, and there might be something inside which shouldn't get wet."

"It's full of big lumps," she said, as they went back into the farmhouse.

Tom cut off the top edge with a pair of scissors as Sheila held the package. She then began placing its contents onto the table. There were two small bricks of what appeared to be pressed sawdust, in clear plastic wrappers. Tom picked one up and examined it. He saw "CEREAL FOOD BAR" printed on one side, and the back of the bar had three grooves molded into it, apparently so the bar could be broken into quarters.

"These look yummy," she said sarcastically, holding up two silver-colored packets.

Tom took them, and saw "PROTEIN PASTE" printed on them. "You'd better hope it's not mashed sardines." There were no other markings. "I guess the aliens aren't into the nutritional-information thing."

"What's this?" Sheila asked, handing over an angular lump of metal with a bulge in the middle and what appeared to be a pipe fitting on one end.

Tom observed three stamped-metal wings on it, and began to unfold them. "I know what this is," he said. "It's a backpacker's camp stove." He held the three spread wings upward, and the fitting downward. "The fitting screws onto a gas bottle, and the three wings hold a pan."

Sheila was reading a piece of white plastic she'd taken out of the package.

"Here you go," she said, handing it over.

"Just great. More fun facts, I'm sure." He put the sheet on the table, surprised at his lack of curiosity about a message from aliens.

"And this must be the gas bottle."

Printed on its side was "COOKING GAS," with nothing else. It was less than half the size of the propane bottles they'd been using. *So the fuel ration wasn't very impressive,* he thought. He screwed the backpacking stove onto the gas bottle.

"And matches. That's all there is."

He placed the backpacker's stove on the table and took the matches she offered. The stove had a tiny knob, which he turned slightly until he heard a faint hissing noise. He opened the packet of cheap paper matches, tore one out, struck it, and moved it slowly to the side of the backpacking stove. As soon as the match was between two of the wings, it lit with a pop. He shook the match out and turned the knob up. The stove blew a noisy blue flame. He turned it back down to a low setting, with barely any flame at all.

"It looks good," he said. "The low setting should be good for simmering rice." Then he remembered there were only about two pounds of brown rice left.

"I'd rather have some tea, I think," Sheila said. She dipped a saucepan into a kitty litter bucket of untreated water they'd been using. It wouldn't cause their drinks to taste like bleach.

"Good idea. Looks like we'd better have drinks ready for these cereal bars."

She handed the pan to Tom, who balanced it on the three wings. Then he turned the stove up to a blowtorch blast, and the pan began to heat quickly. In just a few minutes, the water boiled, quiet was restored with the stove off, and the tea was ready.

"Let's split one," Tom said, holding up a cereal bar. He tried to flex the unopened package, but the bar wouldn't break. So he held it with its middle groove upward at the edge of the table with one hand, and gave the overhanging half a thump with the heel of his other hand. The bar snapped, but plastic wrapper didn't break, so he pulled out his clip knife and cut the pieces apart.

"Bon appétit," Tom said, handing one half to Sheila.

"Do you think they'd poison us?" She took it, after a moment's delay.

Tom tried to think of a diplomatic answer.

"Given our food situation, we'll have to try them sooner or later. Probably sooner." He realized that statement hadn't sweetened the medicine any. But she seemed more focused on her half of the cereal bar than listening to him.

"I'll go first, if you want," Tom said.

"No, we should eat together."

Tom leaned to her, gave her a little kiss, and then tried his half. It tasted of corn and oats, was mildly sweet, and wasn't easy to chew. The vitamin-enriched, preservative-powered aftertaste came quickly and heavily.

"This is almost as hard as a rock," she said. "Were we supposed to soak these things first?"

"Who knows? Were there instructions on the sheet?"

"Read it. You'll love it. More rules."

Tom sat down at the table with his tea and his half of the cereal bar and began reading. He found it difficult to focus on the material, which was mostly about how humans had to be protected from each other. It was nonsense anyway. Foremost in his mind was the concern that they were being issued starvation rations.

By the middle of April, their daily routine was settling into place. The declining quality and quantity of their diet meant that every day's focus was on food. Carrying water for the day was always the first chore, then a quick, standing wash in the bathtub. They would share a cereal bar for breakfast, with a little dried venison and some peppermint tea. Wild peppermint had been growing behind the back yard for years, and boiling water poured over crushed tops of the young plants made a flavorful drink.

Then they would work on the garden. Tom was finishing a strong fence, hoping to keep deer and rabbits out at night. They both spent some time turning the soil, but that was getting done only gradually. Sheila took the lead in laying out the garden, arranging where the various plants would be and transplanting whatever was available.

The shortage of seeds was a huge problem. Tom had traded some .40 S&W pistol ammunition for six seeds each of peas, beans, and corn. They hoped they could save most of their yield for next year's seeds.

Meanwhile, most of the garden would be native plants and whatever else became available. There were a few pumpkin sprouts by the front porch, which were carefully transplanted into the garden. Sheila also transplanted wild garlic, plantain, and burdock sprouts from the old pasture, and hoped to find some chicory also. She decided dandelions wouldn't be transplanted because they had such long tap roots. So she planned to gather some leaves from them wherever they grew wild, and then gather seeds for the garden as the plants matured.

Tom and Sheila knew that the native plants wouldn't provide many calories, but they hoped their efforts would be worthwhile for vitamins, flavoring, and general variety in their diets. The latter was important, as their rations were extremely monotonous. There were always two packets of protein paste, which stunk of fish, liver, or both. Packets of wheat flour sometimes replaced the cereal bars, but the flour wasn't as welcome. The shortage of other ingredients usually meant it had to be mixed with only salt and enough water to form a batter. Then the batter was fried with just a drop of oil to make hardtack discs.

Then, later every morning, it would be time to wait at the mailbox. They always wore hats, but the warming weather made it less practical to limit visibility to their faces. Eventually, concern about being recognized faded away.

At midday, they'd eat whatever wild plant leaves Sheila gathered as a salad, with Tom's soup of the day. When their pre-invasion food ran out, Tom would make soup from any kind of meat available. After a few weeks, he no longer told her what was in the soup, and she stopped asking.

Afternoons were for heavier, more time-consuming chores, such as gathering firewood. Tom began to find, repair, and sharpen old hand tools. Gasoline was quickly running out. So a rusting bow saw in the old silo shed was a huge find.

By sundown, suppertime was very welcome. They had their largest meal of the day then, to make it easier to sleep. They'd divide a cereal bar or hardtack, to have with a packet of protein paste. Those were eaten cold to make the stuff less nauseating. A mug of hot broth or soup to wash it down helped also.

There were meetings Tuesday and Thursday nights in the old church across from the lower end of the farm. Religious topics quickly gave way to more practical matters, such as classes and trading sessions. The classes were taught by volunteers. Old-timers and anyone else having books containing practical information were very welcome. The Tuesday meetings and swap meets were mostly for women, and popular classes included identifying edible native plants, soapmaking from wood ash and animal fat, first aid, gardening, weapons, clothing repair, and water purification. On Thursday nights, mostly men would gather for their swap meet and classes on meat preservation, use of traps and snares, home maintenance, tool sharpening and repair, and fire starting.

The meeting nights had become popular only after the split schedule was devised, to allow someone to remain on guard in every home during the evenings.

The afternoon of April 28, Tom saw Mark Weston carrying buckets toward the well and went out to ask about more seeds for the garden.

"What's the latest, Mark?" he asked, approaching the well.

"I was about to knock on your door before I drew some water. We should talk."

"About what?"

Mark looked around and saw more people approaching. "Let's walk around your house."

"Sure. We have some chairs under the maple tree."

They removed some leaves and twigs from the plastic chairs, then relaxed in the shade of the tree.

"No one at the well can hear us from here," Tom said. "So what's up?"

"Don Simmons is forming a defense committee. Four of us are on it so far and we'd like you to join. We need anyone with military experience."

"As in defense from the aliens?"

"Yeah."

"I'm interested. But I wonder about the intent of this. We're not in a position to do much about the aliens. What are their vulnerabilities? Do they have any? Has anyone even seen a real live alien?"

"Not that I've heard. Just their machines."

"That's probably not a coincidence. It seems they don't intend to expose their vulnerabilities."

"Maybe so. Who knows? What if the delivery truck breaks down?"

"Yeah, who knows? Did Don mention any ideas about what we'd actually do?"

"When we last met, he talked about two things. First, he wants to organize a resistance, an inactive resistance at first. The idea would be to take a count of weapons and ammo available and who might be willing and able to use them in a later phase."

"There can't be much in the valley beyond hunting rifles, some shotguns, and maybe some assorted handguns. What else would there be?"

"Might be more. Maybe we should take a count and see what there is."

"Sure, I get that. It's not a bad idea. Finding out who's willing to support a resistance might be most important. What's the second part?"

"He wasn't specific, but he wants to plan for isolating the valley from the aliens. For example, he said if we wanted to, we could start a rockslide onto Hayes Gap Road and block it. You know how it is down the gap. Rocks are always falling down on the road anyway."

"We could definitely block the road. It would be easier than keeping it open this coming winter. But why? Did he have any kind of strategy for when and why we'd want to do that?"

"No, not that he told me. In fact, that's why I wanted to get you involved in this. Before we start any kind of resistance, we have to have a plan."

"No shit! Otherwise we'd just cut off delivery of what little food we're getting!"

"I had the same thought. Anyway, you're invited. Tomorrow evening at sundown at my place, in the back yard. I'll have a fire going. And I believe the moon will be full, or almost full, for people to walk home."

"Okay, I'll be there. But I have a bad feeling about this."

"I do too. But let's meet and talk. Maybe we can steer clear of bad ideas, if nothing else. For now, I need to get back to the house with some water. See ya."

"Sure. I'll be there," said Tom, already lost in thought. And Mark left, without being asked if he'd heard about anyone with seeds to trade.

Tom was thinking about dental hygiene as he and Sheila waited for the delivery truck the next morning. "There has to be some way to make toothpaste," he said. "My mouth feels like a sewer!"

"I could wash it out with lye soap, like your parents must have done many times."

"Very funny. But right now, I think I'd give it a try."

The now-familiar chirping announced the truck approaching.

"Smile for the camera," Tom said humorlessly.

"Don't even joke about that. You'd better hope there's no camera in that truck!"

With the usual speedy approach and sudden stop, the robot quickly deposited a sheaf into the mailbox. Then the truck sped away.

Tom was surprised. "Did you see that? That was no package!"

"Yes, I saw."

Tom walked to the mailbox, pulled out a small page of white plastic, and read from it:

NOTICE

In accordance with the original declaration of a state of emergency, and the prohibition of weapons contained therein, the following announcement is made:

Yesterday, the driver of this vehicle observed a human displaying a weapon at the top of Pitzer Ridge. As a result, ration deliveries on this route are suspended for three days. During the suspension, you must present yourselves to be counted every day, as previously mandated.

"It's a bunch of crap!" Tom shouted, as he handed the plastic to Sheila.

She read it, and said, "Could it have been someone hunting?"

"No! How could it be? No one lives on Pitzer's Ridge. And who would walk all the way up into the middle of nowhere to hunt, too far away to drag a deer back to their house? And who has so much food they can afford to be wandering around on Pitzer's Ridge while the truck's coming around?"

"So they made it up?"

"They must have. It can't be right!"

"Why would they?"

"I don't know. But from the start, it seems like they've had to provide some bogus justification for everything they're doing. It stinks of politics! Or did they somehow hear about the Hayes Gap scheme?"

Sheila wanted to change the subject. "Come in. I'll fix lunch," she said.

"Yeah, thanks." Tom knew he needed to get his head back in the game. "We still have ten cereal bars we put away while we were finishing the food in the house. We'll be fine."

"I know." Sheila gave him a hug, and they walked back to the house.

After lunch and carrying in some water, Tom's concern about the ration suspension was still growing.

"Sheila, I'm going to walk down to the Westons'. I want to talk about that Pitzer Ridge thing. I wonder if maybe there was someone scouting around through the hills, especially after hearing about that hare-brained Hayes Gap plan."

"I'm still interested in some seeds for the garden. An old potato that's sprouting out would be good too. Tell 'em they can have any of your old stuff in trade!"

"How generous of me," Tom said, going out the back door.

Walking from the back yard into the former corn field, now full of wild grasses and weeds, Tom noticed that the line for the well was longer than ever. But everything was orderly and there was no cause for concern. So he focused on crossing the field to the road, picking his way through the clumps of weeds. The road made for easier walking, since it had become only an extra-wide sidewalk. He was soon a half-mile from the house, where he saw Mark Weston coming the opposite way, carrying two empty five-gallon buckets on a shoulder pole.

"Needing water?" Tom asked.

"Oh yeah."

"I was coming to talk, so I'll walk with you back to my house, if you don't mind."

"About the ration suspension, I assume."

"Yeah. Do you happen to know if anyone was scouting around along Hayes Gap or Pitzer Ridge?"

"Ha! That's been the hot topic on my end today, too. Some people are raising hell about it! But no one seems to know anything definite. Don Simmons said he had nothing to do with it. Maybe he did and he's denying it because people are so mad, but I don't think so. It doesn't make much sense anyway. Who'd walk all the way out to Pitzer Ridge, and for what?"

"I told Sheila about the same thing. I think the aliens are lying about seeing someone up on the ridge. But why would they?"

They walked for a while, with the question hanging.

"Would you want to walk on top of Pitzer Ridge?" Mark asked.

"Oh, hell no. It's all slate, isn't it? I'm sure you could get up there somehow, but I wouldn't want to walk on so much loose slate. There must a thousand places where a person might slide down."

"So let's say they lied. Why would they?"

"I've thought about that some. One: Maybe they're short on rations and are trying to stretch their supply. But I don't think so. It seems they have full control of everything. Two: Maybe they just don't want to issue rations. I'm not sure what to believe."

"Let's think about that possibility," Mark said.

"They want to demonstrate they have the power to deny rations? They want to exhaust any reserve supplies we might have? The truck-driving robot wants a few days off to go to the beach?"

"Maybe they want to incite people to protest or resist in some way. Or see if they will."

"That's possible," Tom said. "Maybe we've been too docile and they think the situation is too quiet."

"Docile. That's a hell of a thing. Who would have expected it to turn out like this? But what's there to do?"

They walked quietly for a while, approaching the well and Tom's house.

"I don't know what to suggest," Tom said. "And I can't imagine what might be behind holding back the rations. But everyone sure will be lined up for 'em the day we get fed again."

"We're supposed to be lined up every day until then anyway. But I agree, everyone will definitely be waiting when the rations come again. Could that be the thing behind all this?"

"I don't see how."

"Me either. But I could think better on a full belly and without sore feet."

"Mark, I don't want to mess with the defense committee thing tonight."

"I don't want to either. And with the heat on Simmons now, rightly or wrongly, I doubt he's much interested in it at the moment. So when I get back, I'll tell him tonight's meeting is canceled."

"Thanks, Mark."

"Sure. I'd better get in line for the well now. See you around."

"See ya," Tom said, forgetting the seeds again.

✦ ✦ ✦

Three days later, Tom and Sheila were waiting for the truck at the usual time.

"I hope there are no more problems," Tom said. "Our food reserve is the lowest it's been."

"Don't worry. The garden is off to a good start."

Tom's morale sunk further. He'd never tell Sheila, but the garden was a huge disappointment, compared to the lush gardens they'd had there when he was young. Most of the plants they were growing now would have been considered weeds. He thought of the old garden, with huge green peppers he could pick and eat immediately. And the full rows of potatoes, onions, and cabbages. And the sweet corn, when so much became ripe that he could eat as much as he wanted with every meal and there would still be corn left over. Then he realized his belly was doing his thinking for him.

"I've got to focus," he said aloud.

"We're doing fine; don't worry so much," Sheila said.

"I haven't been thinking ahead enough."

"We've been busy with our daily chores. Don't beat yourself up."

"Do you know what 'the initiative' means, as in military usage?"

"No," Shelia said, with a little annoyance. "You're the military expert!"

"No, I'm not. No one seems to be. And that's a problem. The initiative means having enough control of the situation to do, or to try to do, whatever you want."

"Like when you wrecked my car!"

"Not funny. But at that point, we had enough initiative to escape from the situation and get here."

"I'm glad we did. Thank you for that. Seriously."

"The problem since then…," Tom said, looking up the road, the direction in which the delivery truck would approach, "…is that we've been totally reactive. We've lost the initiative. Now the aliens can sit back and plan anything they want to do, then give it a try. We haven't even found a way to resist."

"What should we do?"

Tom paused, and shook his head. "I just don't know. The aliens have obviously done this kind of thing before, or they studied long and hard how to control us. Both, maybe. Who knows? But I feel like I've missed something important."

"Let's just focus on what we're doing and get ready for winter. I'll get fat if you get fat!"

Tom laughed a little, as they began to hear the truck's chirping.

"That sounds like the best plan yet!"

The truck approached quickly and slowed suddenly, as always. But the robot held only the gun, nothing to deliver. There were two crackling snaps and the truck sped away. Tom fell to his knees, blood flowing from his chest. He had been cut open from the left side, and his left arm had fallen to the ground separately. Sheila was already down. The gun was too quiet for any of the neighbors to hear, and it didn't even produce a visible beam of light. Tom knew that the neighbors would have no warning. He fell next to Sheila, into some of her blood.

She was silently gasping for breath, but it was hopeless. Her silent gasps were fading. Tom wanted to move, to comfort her, but he couldn't. He could only stare into her eyes, and realize how easily they'd been deceived.

As he died, he knew he was part of a thoroughly conquered people.

www.ingramcontent.com/pod-product-compliance
Lightning Source LLC
LaVergne TN
LVHW041630060526
838200LV00040B/1518